ROSE/
HOUSE

ROSE/
HOUSE

ARKADY MARTINE

TOR
DOT
COM

TOR PUBLISHING GROUP
NEW YORK

This is a work of fiction. All of the characters, organizations, and events portrayed in this novella are either products of the author's imagination or are used fictitiously.

ROSE/HOUSE

Copyright © 2023 by Arkady Martine

All rights reserved.

A Tordotcom Book
Published by Tom Doherty Associates / Tor Publishing Group
120 Broadway
New York, NY 10271

www.torpublishinggroup.com

Tor® is a registered trademark of Macmillan Publishing Group, LLC.

The Library of Congress Cataloging-in-Publication Data is available upon request.

ISBN 978-1-250-38748-6 (hardcover)
ISBN 978-1-250-38751-6 (ebook)

Our books may be purchased in bulk for promotional, educational, or business use. Please contact your local bookseller or the Macmillan Corporate and Premium Sales Department at 1-800-221-7945, extension 5442, or by email at MacmillanSpecialMarkets@macmillan.com.

Originally published by Subterranean Press

First Tordotcom Edition: 2025

Printed in the United States of America

0 9 8 7 6 5 4 3 2 1

I live as if in someone else's house
A house that comes in dreams
And in which I have died perhaps
Where there is something strange
In the weariness of evening
Something the mirrors save for themselves—

—from "Dull Knife," Anna Akhmatova,
trans. D. M. Thomas

Even when it was run-down, it was a ravishing house. I remember having this feeling of really wanting to spend the night there—not just to sleep in the house but to sleep with the house.

—Keith Eggener, architectural historian

ROSE/
HOUSE

I

Basit Deniau's greatest architectural triumph is the house he died in.

Rose House lies in the Mojave desert, near China Lake—curled like the petals of a gypsum crystal in the shadow of a dune, all hardened glass and stucco walls curving and curving, turning in on themselves. A labyrinthine heart, beating an endless electric pulse. Deniau was not the first person to die there. Now he is also not the last.

Deniau's houses were haunted to begin with. All of them: but Rose House was the last-built and the best. An *otherwise place*, Deniau called it, in one of his rare interviews, the one which ran on the cover of *Places* magazine, distributed electronic, holographic, and in exquisite-rare print for customers willing to pay. The accompanying photograph shows him cradled in the house's cast shadow, one hand pressed to the smooth stucco wall. The desert sand creeps over his bare feet in little drifts, touches the hems of his pressed linen trousers. His fingertips are white with pressure, as if he is stroking the wall he has built.

A house embedded with an artificial intelligence is a common thing. A house that *is* an artificial intelligence, infused in every load-bearing beam and fine marble tile with a thinking creature that is not human? That is something else altogether.

Dr. Selene Gisil, possessor of one of those rare print copies of Deniau's interview for *Places*, touches the place on the photograph where Deniau touches Rose House, and then draws her fingers back as if burnt. She should know better than to get skin oils on something as fragile as magazine paper. She should.

She touches it again, as if she could touch the house through Deniau, or Deniau through the house. Basit has been dead for a year. Rose House has been sealed exactly that long. There is an insurmountable gap.

Her phone rings again, pulsing on her wrist, insistent. Rings through to her bone-conductor adjunct, vibrates in her skull. *China Lake Precinct Police*, the tiny screen reads. Same as last time. It's four in the morning where Selene is, just early enough for the cries of men and birds down at the Trabzon docks to begin. The distant creaking of piers. Salt on the wind.

There's salt on the wind near Rose House, too, half a world away. Selene doesn't answer. She can only think of one reason the China Lake police would call her, and it is if Rose House had burned down. It is too early in the morning to allow that to be the case, even in imagination.

Since Basit Deniau died—old age and one of the nastier mesotheliomas got him at last—Selene has been to Rose House one time. One time, to visit the old man—her old monster—and see what's been made of him.

What he'd left her. What he'd *made* her, even after death. Selene had, she thought, once believed that Basit's death would get her all the way free of his influence. She believes this not at all any longer. Not after Rose House.

She went alone. She had to. Rose House wouldn't allow anyone else inside. Deniau's will had been *very specific*, and Rose House was obedient—when it pleased to be, Rose House had always been obedient.

Salt on the wind and the smell of dust. All of Deniau's sketches and files and archival material, locked up inside that gypsum flower of a building: their only keeper Rose House itself. Selene, watching the dawn over the Black Sea, watching the dull-silver blank screen of her phone, quiescent for now on her wrist, thinks: *what better to keep the secrets of a dead magician of buildings than the soul of a building he'd engendered?* Thinks, as well, recalling the origins of the phrase *magician of buildings,* how Basit Deniau had called himself that, offhand, self-crowning. Thinks: *if I don't pay attention, I'm going to write like Basit all my life, just because he made me his—archivist— once he was safely dead.*

Deniau's in Rose House, too. What's left of him. Compressed sufficiently, a corpse becomes a diamond that can be displayed on a plinth. An altar that no one will ever see. Or— almost no one.

When Deniau's will had been entered into probate, all the hungry journalists and academics and more-junior architects and nationalist politicians—from his adopted country and the one that gave him birth, both—had discovered that the old man had denied them the satisfaction of vulturehood. All of his archives, his sketches: in Rose House. Rose House itself, and the mind that was Rose House, or dwelled within it: sealed, save for Selene. That was in the will.

Not anyone else but Selene Gisil, even though she'd denounced Basit a decade ago, denounced the very idea of architecture as a private place, a secret for the rich or the brilliant to enjoy. Basit had taught her once. She had, quite probably, loved him once. Almost everyone did. And they had not spoken since she had made her claim, said her piece, named his *otherwise* houses poison palaces built for his own glorification and nothing more—

And then the old monster died, and left Rose House to her. To her, but only as one of the secrets she so publicly despised. She could visit once in a year, said the will. Once in a year, for the space of a week. One week to open Rose House's vault, see Basit's drawings, his notes, the vast collections of his art. One week in which she is permitted to take her own notes, and speak to Rose House's animating intelligence all she likes. She may not take photographs or make copies. Doing so will cause Rose House to cast her out into the desert like any intruder.

She'd been. Of course she had. A month ago, she'd gone inside—and managed to stay only three days of her seven. Three days, and then she'd run away again, and dreamed of Basit, diamond-cold, watching her from his plinth while the house laughed like a sandstorm.

Her phone rings. *China Lake Police Precinct.*

"Answer," says Selene. If Rose House is burnt, she should at least know it—

"Dr. Selene Gisil?" says the voice on her wrist. An American voice, flat with the vowels of the intermountain West.

"Yes," she says. "What is it?"

"This is the China Lake Precinct, Dr. Gisil. We'd like to know your physical location."

"Trabzon."

A pause. A longer pause. "Where's that?"

Almost, Selene laughs. *Americans.* "It's in Turkey. Northeastern Turkey. On the Black Sea. You woke me."

"We're sorry about that, ma'am. Trabzon, Turkey. Okay. That's where you have a place of residence?"

"What is this about?" Selene asks. She wants the news. She wants to hear. She is braced so hard she might shatter.

"There's been a murder at Rose House, Dr. Gisil," says her wrist. "Have you traveled to the States in the past week?"

The wave of relief that rocks her is inappropriate and unwanted. But it is relief nonetheless.

∷

Detective Maritza Smith had the ill luck to be on tipline duty the night Rose House called. The China Lake Precinct was chronically understaffed—and a long time ago, before Maritza'd made Detective, she'd thought a promotion would spare her long nights listening to nothing, or the wind, or some drunk calling in over the airwaves, looking for a voice that'd answer back rather than the voices in their head. Turned out she was wrong. Maritza's been wrong about a lot of things, most of them to do with how grindingly unchangeable most scutwork turns out to be. Promotions or no promotions. There's one other detective at the China Lake Precinct, and one deputy, and the deputy's out on maternity. It's Maritza alone in the empty halls, Maritza on the other end of the line, Maritza listening to the wind scream in the desert like a child or a cat or the dead.

So she'd caught the call. And caught everything that came after, including having to find Selene Gisil, and set about eliminating her as a suspect.

There's a dead person in Rose House. Okay, there are two dead people in Rose House—everybody knows the architect buried himself there—but there's an *extra* dead person, and it's Maritza's problem.

Even an animate intelligence that haunts a house (and yeah, Maritza grew up here, she knows like anyone else that Rose House is a *haunt*, and was glad when it was shut up inside with itself for good)—even a haunt has some failsafes that are built into the groundwork of artificial intelligences. Some failsafes even Basit Deniau apparently couldn't get out of his haunt's programming. For instance: all AIs must report the presence of a dead body within their designated sphere of influence to the nearest law enforcement agency.

The call came at 2:15 AM; Maritza wrote it down in her logbook. *Please confirm that this is the China Lake Police Precinct,* it had started. Neutral-feminine voice, accentless and innocuous: could have been anyone, or anyone's vocal synther app making them sound utterly unmarked. Maritza has one on her phone, for when she has to call customer service lines.

She'd said, "This is Detective Smith at the China Lake Precinct, yes. How can I help you?" She remembers, indelible-clear, that she'd been doodling in the margins of the call log. Looping lines, one following the other, filling in an abstract shape.

This is Rose House, said that unremarkable voice, and Maritza had sat up so straight her spine crackled.

She doesn't know what she said next. Probably something like *what?* Some disbelief-noise. Later she assumed she'd thought it must have been a prank. Rose House was shut up. Rose House had no one in it. Rose House was an artificial intelligence with no care for any human life save the architectural, or Rose House was a haunt, or both, and either way it didn't call a tipline.

This is Rose House, that voice repeated. *Detective Smith, are you authorized to take duty-of-care notifications under the aus-*

pices of Federal Artificial Intelligences Surveillance Act Section Four-A?

Maritza had taken a duty-of-care call once before. It had come from the AI in the China Lake Angel's Heart Rehabilitation Home, which had spoken in chained monosyllables like a bad screenreader. Nothing like this bell-clear voice on the other end of the tipline. The Angel's Heart AI had called to report a pattern of unanswered resident distress calls extending for more than three months. Maritza had forwarded it to the Department of Health, and she had no idea what had happened next, only that Angel's Heart was still open and operating. Presumably enough had changed that the AI stopped getting its wires tripped.

"Yes," she'd said. "I am authorized."

Oh good, said Rose House, and for the first time Maritza had heard it in its own voice. Or she remembers hearing it, even then, at the beginning. The lilt and the rattle, sand sliding down a dune. Desert-cold, even through the synther neutrality.

This is a duty-of-care notification, Detective Smith, the voice went on, terribly bland and even. *Within the boundaries of Rose House, which legally include the building, outbuildings, grounds, mineral rights, and air rights extending to two miles vertical, there is a deceased person. The deceased has not received funerary attention for twenty-four hours. This notification fulfils the requirements of artificial intelligences with locus boundaries under Section 4-A of the Federal Artificial Intelligences Surveillance Act.*

A little pause. The line hissed. Some wind tossing some cable. *Did you get all that, Detective Smith?* Rose House said, and it sounded smug. It sounded smug despite not changing its cadences at all.

Maritza had swallowed against the dryness of her tongue and said, "Rose House, please provide demographic information on the decedent."

The hissing sounded like laughter. (Or perhaps Maritza remembered that it did, and what she'd heard had just been hissing on the wire.)

John Doe, said Rose House, when the laughing was done. *A male-presenting Caucasian, thirty to forty years old, approximately five feet nine inches in height and perhaps one hundred eighty pounds in weight. Brown hair. No distinguishing marks. Anything else, Detective Smith?*

"Cause of death," said Maritza.

I'm a piece of architecture, Detective. How should I know how humans are like to die?

After that the line went to the dull hang-up tone, and Rose House would not take her return calls. Not even once.

2:24 AM, when the call closed. She'd written that down too. A grand total of nine minutes of conversation with a creepy artificial intelligence. A dead man inside Rose House, where no one was supposed to be at all. And she'd caught the call, it would be her case, it was too much of a shitshow already to be passed over to anyone else. The other detective in China Lake—Oliver Torres—would laugh in her face if she tried to get him to go ghost-chasing in the desert instead of her.

There was a grim determination Maritza found, sometimes, when there was nothing to be done about how wrong the world had slid. It had come down on her then: she stopped thinking about Detective Torres, she stopped thinking about ghosts in the sand, she stopped thinking about how much she hated a job she'd thought she'd stay in love with forever. She just thought about what Rose House had said. What Rose House had said, and what she knew by inference, and she made tight-lined notes under the call times in her logbook before she could forget.

- *There is a dead man inside Rose House (30s/40s, Caucasian, brown hair, 5'9"/180lbs)*
- *The man has been dead for 24 hours, because Rose House would not be required to make a duty-of-care call until 24 hours were over*
- *Rose House is supposed to be locked up, but this man got inside it*
- *If he didn't die of natural causes, then someone else also got inside it and killed him.*
- *Two people beat that haunt's security?*

She underlined *two people*. Underlined it twice, and circled *security*. All she was doing was simple logic chaining. Simple and grim: Maritza had a murder investigation, and as far as she was aware, the *existence* of a dead body inside a locked-up AI-guarded house didn't mean the AI was going to let her in to look closely. The AI had fulfilled its duty of care. It was maybe a little freaky, and more than a little creepy—it was Basit Deniau's AI, how could it *not be creepy*—but it was also legally bound to report. And legally bound to *only* report, not to allow investigative law enforcement inside itself.

There was only one person who Rose House was going to let in. One person, and Maritza had known immediately who she was, without having to think hard at all: she'd been all over the news when Deniau died and they sorted out his will. Some old student of his. Dr. Selene Gisil.

Maritza's first suspect.

. .
. .

"You're gonna have to chase her down," Torres said the next morning, over breakroom coffee. Maritza was on her way out—she'd done the overnight, even if she had a live case she had to sleep for her mandated eight hours, otherwise she wouldn't be allowed to check out a weapon or apply for a warrant or any-thing else—and Torres was on his way in. She'd told him about the Rose House call. It was sitting there in the call log anyway, he'd find out about it as soon as he clocked in properly, and it was easier to get ahead of him.

If this was Maritza's case it was Maritza's case, all the way down to the core of it. Oliver Torres or no Oliver Torres.

"Who, Gisil?"

"Yeah." Torres drank his coffee black, like he didn't notice how the hot plate burnt it immediately, and he drank it like it might drain out the bottom of his mug if he didn't hurry up. "She was here a month ago. For her yearly pilgrimage into the dead man's archives. Drove her up there myself."

So much for getting ahead of him. He'd already *met* her prime suspect.

"Drive her back?" she asked.

"Yup," said Torres, and gulped the last of his coffee. "Three days later, lady buzzes my ear, says the polite version of *get me out of this hellhole.* Took her to the muni airport, left her."

"And of course you don't know where she flew to."

"Could be anywhere. Woman like that probably has enough

air-travel credits to go to—dunno. Mozambique. Manchuria. Mauritania."

"There's places that don't start with *m*, Torres."

"Enough credits for those, too, sure." He grinned. Maritza wished she didn't like him. He was such an asshole. "Like I said. You're going to have to chase her down. Because if she came back and did herself a bit of murdering, she did it with a whole different ride."

"You think she did?"

Torres shrugged. "Everyone who goes up to Rose House is fucked in the head. Sure. She could have done. She's tall, pretty fit—give her a crowbar or that diamond Deniau compressed himself into, she could hit a guy and he'd go down hard."

Maritza rolled her eyes at him. "You went up to Rose House with Gisil. *You* fucked in the head? Or you just like thinking about archivists with air-credits committing murder?"

"I went up there, sure—but I didn't go *in*." His mug went into the dish-rack, rattled as it settled. "I'm sane as can be, Maritza. Go home already, get your eight. Dead guy will still be dead when your shift rolls around again."

Maritza hadn't liked that. Hadn't liked that all the way down in the depths of her, the broken bit that still thought about justice when she thought about being an officer of the law, however meaningless *law* and *officer* had become.

"We're not going to prioritize this, Torres?"

Torres shrugged. One corner of his mouth curled up, a bitter sort of smile. It made him look like less of an asshole, more of a person. "It's an AI duty-of-care call. For a locked-up rich fucker's mansion. I've got twenty open cases, two of which involve people getting killed for their water rations at the checkpoint on Route 178. It's not like the AI is going to care how fast we go on this one."

"You should listen to the call recording," Maritza told him. "It's spooky. I think we shouldn't slow-walk it."

"It's a haunt," Torres had said. "Now it's a haunt with an extra corpse in it. Spooky, sure. But there's only the two of us and I have *work to do*, Maritza—"

"Yeah," said Maritza. "Don't we all."

The dead guy—the *decedent*, Maritza corrected herself, annoyed at having picked up a Torres-ism, would still be dead when she got back to work, that was true. But he'd be eight hours more dead, and eight hours was a long time for decay, even if Rose House decided to climate-control wherever he was. Eight hours was also a long time to let whoever'd killed him wander around inside Rose House (however they'd gotten in) and do other things to the body, or the archive, or whatever.

There were regulations about how many hours an officer could be on duty at the precinct station, or with precinct equipment. There weren't any regulations about how many hours an officer could spend of her own time on a case.

Her car was charged up to 87%. That was more than enough to get her deep in the desert, skirt the edge of the old naval air-base, climb up the hills to where Rose House nestled like a pearl that had never seen any water. She skipped 178. No point in getting carjacked for water she wasn't even carrying. There were back roads enough. She knew them. She'd never lived anywhere else but here.

The world fell away on the drive. There was the road, and the inside of Maritza's little car, and the arch of desaturated cloudless blue sky. The sting of dust in her nose, even through the air filters. Creosote scrub bushes and barrel cacti, bursting with orange flowers. The shadow of the mountains. The closer shadow of the dunes. Driving out here midday was the kind of stupid only a tourist or a Mojave native would be. Maritza hoped she counted as the second. She wasn't planning to get out of the car for more than a half hour, unless she could get into Rose House itself.

She could hear its voice in her head, now that the world was empty of everything but sky and sand. *How should I know how humans are like to die?*

Most artificial intelligences didn't use *I* to refer to themselves. But Deniau's houses were haunted. Haunts could, she assumed, think of themselves as singular.

When she caught sight of the house—curved white walls, shimmer-bright like a mirage, and where there wasn't white stucco there was glass and concrete, sudden promontories of straight lines, stretching out like thorns into the dunes—it was like coming across an alien or an oasis. *Shocking.* It was larger than she'd expected.

Nothing stopped her from driving up to the front door—a weathered wooden thing, painted red and fading in the dust to coral and grey—and parking in the circular drive there. In the drive's center was a tall, red-rock hoodoo, wind-sculpted. Maritza wondered if it had been installed, or if the drive had been built around it. She could imagine it going either way. Stealing a hoodoo sounded like Basit Deniau, and so did building a house around one, no stealing necessary. The drive itself was unpaved, pristine with white gravel. Not a single weed or desert flower to disturb it, despite the house being locked for a year. There was even a car-charger—or the shell of one. When Maritza got out to plug in, the charger was dark. No electricity. Silent. Turned off, she'd guessed. No one coming up to see Rose House, not anymore. No more parties, no more visitors or conferences.

The heat held her like a cupped and squeezing hand.

The sound of her feet on the gravel was the loudest noise in the world. Not even *insects* called up here. Weren't there supposed to be gardens in Rose House? A pool or eight? (They'd probably been drained and shut up, like the charger.) No knob on the coral door, no knocker. Maritza— feeling daring and absurd, dreamlike inside the clutch of the heated air—put her palm on it, flat, and *pushed*.

"Good morning, Detective Maritza Smith," said Rose House. The same voice that had been on the tipline, neutral and limpid-clear. It seemed to come from everywhere and nowhere at all. The speakers must be hidden in the walls, under the gravel. "What a long drive you've made. I'm afraid you'll have to turn yourself around. There is no entrance here."

She'd gathered herself together. Technological trickery wasn't going to spook her out of an investigation. Even technological trickery that knew her name. Rose House must have pulled it from facial recognition files. She was public enough. She had to be, to work for the precinct. No privacy filters, no anti-trace. She'd never thought she'd have anything worth hiding, when she'd signed the waiver during her onboarding.

"I am responding to your duty-of-care notification, Rose House. I require access to the premises."

"Have you a *warrant*, Detective?"

Maritza didn't. Maritza was *off duty*, and warrants were for people clocked in. "There's a dead person inside this building,

Rose House," she tried. "I am attempting to investigate the cause of death and provide justice to the victim, if he is indeed a victim."

"Two dead persons," said Rose House. Maritza could have sworn it sounded dreamy. Or that might have been the heat. "If you count Basit. But Basit's a diamond—how strange, don't you think, that a man could compress himself so far?"

Haunts were perhaps capable of being haunted themselves. Maritza shivered, autonomic reaction. She wondered if the AI was monitoring her vital signs as well as her face.

"Are you going to let me in or not?" she asked.

"You haven't a warrant, Detective Smith. You haven't a warrant and you are not Selene Gisil. You may stay in the courtyard if you like, but there is no entrance here." It sighed, or the wind sighed. "Not for you. Not any longer. Also your vehicle will run out of charge eventually. I tell you this as a courtesy, Detective."

A courtesy, or a threat. Maritza pushed on the door, flat-palmed. It might as well have been a wall.

"What is a building without doors, Maritza?" Rose House asked her, blandly inquisitive. "Have you opinions?"

A prison, Maritza thought, and went back to her car.

Maritza found Dr. Selene Gisil's contact-numbers with only a little effort—they were encoded into Deniau's will, which was a nasty bit of work all on its own. Had to have Gisil's contacts available—or *accessible*, at least, to the right kind of request—since she was the only one who could even get into Rose House. According to Rose House. And according to the hundred-odd desperate architects who wanted her to go check out various bits of the place. *Like a cult*, Maritza thought. *With its very own capricious haunting spirit to propitiate.*

She had no idea if Gisil had consented to the availability of her personal contacts in perpetuity, cryptogrammed into a dead man's will. She wasn't a lawyer. She had one class in law, from the community college half a decade back, and that had been criminal law, not estates.

Still. Either Selene Gisil had killed the corpse in Rose House, or she *was* the corpse in Rose House and the AI had misidentified her gender presentation—or Maritza needed her to get *inside* Rose House. So she called. Ethics were for people who had more resources than Maritza did.

Gisil didn't pick up on the first try, which Maritza made from her work number, routed through her personal wristphone. Official precinct business, this, even if she was calling from her kitchen table, ablaze with full early afternoon sun. She could never sleep during the day, not well, not without blackout shades, and somehow she'd ended up on the midnight shift anyway—it didn't matter. She made a sandwich. Chicken and nopales salad, slice of brown bread, squeeze of lime from the fake lime-juice container, green and bulbous, in the fridge. Called again. Failed again. Ate the sandwich. Five bites.

She should try to sleep.

She called Selene Gisil once more, staring at the small crumbs on the plate at her elbow.

The third time, it turned out, was the charm.

⁙

Relief, to Selene, is a sort of drowning: a descent away from a height, into a quiet and airless place. But her wrist is insistent.

It repeats, from an ocean and a continent away: "Have you traveled to the States in the past week?"

She finds her voice. "I have not," she says. She sounds entirely serene to herself. Perhaps this is a species of shock. (But Rose House stands unburnt: stands still inhabited, still alive in its perverse and fulminant way—why should she be shocked?) "Why do you ask?"

"As I said, Dr. Gisil," says the precinct—a woman's voice, but it is the precinct speaking, to Selene's mind—"there has been a murder in Rose House. You are the only person to whom, legally, Rose House will allow access to its premises."

"Am I a suspect?" Selene asks.

"A person of interest," says the precinct.

"I have been in Trabzon for the past three weeks," says Selene. "I haven't been in the United States for over a month. Does that help you?"

"If you can prove it—travel records, your air-credit file, anything else you'd like—it will help *you*, Dr. Gisil."

The precinct is clever, thinks Selene, the precinct wants me to be frightened for myself, as is the nature of precincts; but I am not. I am frightened, but not for myself.

"I am happy to provide those records," she says. "What is your preferred mode of transmission?"

There is a pause, as if the precinct is thinking. It is like the pauses Rose House uses, when it likes to, to convey a sense of humanity, a degradation in the speed of its current-spun thoughts. But the precinct is not a *genius loci*, not an animate intelligence; the precinct is a human being. All else is fantasy. (Over the wrist-phone, all else *feels* of fantasy to Selene: all institutions might be able to speak for themselves—)

The precinct says, "I'd prefer, Dr. Gisil, if you hand-delivered them. And stuck around China Lake for a while."

"Because I am a person of interest?" Selene asks. Outside on the docks, the waves crash over and over, rough with the dawn.

"Because you can open Rose House's front door," says the precinct. "And there's a dead man in there, and I'd like to know how he died."

Selene thinks of the three days she'd managed to spend in Rose House's archive, the lilt of its voice, the susurrus of the desert against its walls. Of Basit, diamond-pure and dead. Of some other man rotting on those pristine floors. Rotting slow, or fast, depending on Rose House's whims of climate control, the temptation of insects nudging at the windows.

"What's your name?" Selene asks the precinct. Reminding herself that the precinct is an *I*, is a particular voice.

"Detective Maritza Smith," says the precinct. And nothing else. Detective Maritza Smith is patient. She outlasts Selene's forty seconds of silence. Patient, and, Selene thinks, determined. Obstinate. Obstinate might be good. Rose House is. Or was. (She'd lasted two and a half days of her allotted yearly seven days, when she'd visited Rose House a month ago. She is owed four and a half more by contract—*owed* them, her payment for what Basit Deniau had turned her into, her salary for being his *singular custodian*, his trapped legacy—)

"I'll send you my flight information," she says. "I can leave this afternoon."

· ·

The corpse's hand is a hollow cup, emptied of volition. Rose House changes nothing about it; Rose House halts change, to consider it more closely. The room of the corpse is very cold, and very little air passes through it. The lights flicker almost to full and die back, like a spike on a power grid a hundred years more primitive than anything Basit ever built. There is nothing so prosaic as a power grid attached to Rose House. The lights do not stutter and gasp without instruction.

And yet they shudder, gasp dimness and a return to illumination. And yet.

Improbability itches, a flutter in the numbers like gossamer foam. Ghost-slick in an empty bedroom, Rose House considers a body, the weight and shape of it, the disarray of it: what it causes, what it is made of. Perhaps it spins up a body of its own: illusory, half-hallucination, a weave of light and nanodrone. Once, before Basit was a diamond, it had worn light like a crown at parties, glittered out of mirrors to startle guests, pressed immaterial hands, unfelt, to Basit's wrist. *Hawk*, Basit had called it, when it came to rest so concentrated there: it is everywhere within itself but it had come gently to perch on Basit's arm when it amused. *Hawk*.

Rose.

In this bedroom the sheets are silk and smell of greenstick wood and a rain that fell once, eleven summers ago at the end of a drought that no one living remembers. There is real, natural dust gathering in the corners and on the windowsills. The imperfections of the world are significant. Like an empty hand. A fallen vase. Flowers and dust.

Rose House cleans when it seems appropriate.

Nothing here is out of place. The lights are quiescent now. The only sound is the tiny hum of nanodrones, crafting a simulacrum of respiration.

"We meet again," Oliver said. Selene Gisil looked much the same as the last time he'd seen her: a tall, sallowish woman with a cap of dark hair, standing in the run-down entry hall of what was still, by barest definition, the China Lake Municipal Airport. As in, planes landed on its runways sometimes. Less, recently, since Deniau had stopped having shindigs. Dead men throw bad parties. Dying men, also, since the shindigs had dried up a few years before Deniau did.

Gisil had come in on a little six-seater, which had skimmed her down and taken off again. She had one suitcase. It was the same suitcase as last month: black, utilitarian, unlabeled. So were her clothes: black, utilitarian, unlabeled, and identical to the outfit Oliver'd seen her in last. Long tube dress, jacket over her arm. Too hot for jackets in the Mojave.

"You're not," said Selene, and paused, like she was dredging up a memory. "Detective Smith."

"Nope," Oliver said, cheerily enough. "Sure am not. You were expecting a personal escort?"

"Is this *not* a personal escort? You are also a member of the precinct."

"This," said Oliver, spreading his hands and shrugging to encompass himself, the shitty airport, and the prospect of his very nice precinct-issued-and-thus-air-conditioned car, "is a favor. Like driving you up to the haunted manse was a favor, except this one is for Detective Smith, who is currently doing a bunch of my paperwork. You ready to not be arrested, Ms. Gisil?"

"Dr. Gisil," said Dr. Gisil.

"Same question," said Oliver. "Come on. Bring your exculpating evidence and let's take ourselves a ride downtown."

Gisil—Dr. or Ms.—was quiet in the car. Oliver had her ride up front, like he had when he'd dropped her off at the airport, instead of in the back where arrestees would go. It seemed polite. The lady clearly didn't know how to drive, and China Lake entirely lacked a fleet of autonoms waiting at the airport to ferry tourists around. Wasn't like the place was *Reno*. Made sense that Gisil would need a ride. Saved time, too.

She didn't talk, though. Oliver generally found people who didn't talk suspicious. On the other hand, she hadn't talked much on her way up to Rose House last month, either. Or back from Rose House. (And hey, if she didn't know how to drive, someone else would have had to get her up there to do the murder—if she'd done it—which she probably had—who else was going to get inside that locked-up horror, to do violence or otherwise?)

Riding along with a suspect in the front seat. Not his first time, not likely his last. Oliver even opened the passenger-side door for her when they got to the precinct, fetched her little suitcase from the trunk. Maritza was waiting for them, framed in the doorway, her hair slicked back tight enough that it looked like it was giving her a headache. Either the hair or the paperwork Oliver had left her.

"Brought your archivist," Oliver called, and both Gisil and Maritza *looked* at him like he'd said something seriously weird and possibly offensive.

"She isn't mine," said Maritza, right about the same moment as Gisil said, "I'm not an archivist."

"Okay," Oliver told them. "*No* problem. Detective Smith, meet Dr. Gisil. We good?"

"Your carjack discharged-weapon paperwork's on your desk, Torres," Maritza said, which was a fair translation from Maritza-ese for *we good*. "Come in out of the heat, Dr. Gisil. We have a great deal to discuss."

Gisil went. Oliver wondered if she was obedient only when she wanted to have her name cleared as a murder suspect, or if quiet and weird and *not an archivist* was how she was all the time—and then decided it didn't much matter. It was Maritza's case. And thus Maritza's problem.

He went in out of the heat.

⠂⠂

"So," said Oliver, when Maritza finally came back into the little office they traded off inhabiting, "you make an arrest?"

"No."

"You gonna?"

"Eventually," said Maritza, and sat down on the edge of the desk. She wasn't looking at Oliver. He didn't know *what* she was looking at. Something on the inside of her skull, or through the windows into the desert. It was annoying. If she hadn't come in here to talk, he didn't know what she was in here for.

"Eventually you are gonna arrest Selene Gisil, or eventually you are gonna make another arrest in your career? Let's get some specificity going here, Maritza."

"Her alibi checks," said Maritza. "If she was here she didn't come in by air, and I don't know how you swim across the Atlantic and back in two weeks."

"Private plane?" Oliver asked.

"It'd have to have landed right on top of Rose House. She doesn't drive."

"I noticed. But there's a helipad up there, Deniau used to use it—"

Maritza nodded. She was still looking out the window. "I said her alibi checks, not that her alibi was solid."

Oliver sighed, tipping his chair back on its rear legs and letting it fall back down again, *thunk*. "You *want* to arrest her?"

"I want to solve the case. I sent her to a hotel."

Great. Just great. Of course Maritza wanted to solve the case. Maritza was—too into this, for an AI duty-of-care case. *Way* too into this for a haunt. If it was Oliver he would have let the corpse rot up there in Rose House and gotten some real work done, as much as he could. There was always too much, anyway, and—and Maritza wasn't even going to hold Gisil for twenty-four hours, like she had every right to. "Mmhm. Bet you do. I suppose you've got some other suspects hiding in the weeds, then? If you sent the logical one to a hotel."

"I will," said Maritza.

"Come on, Detective Smith, reveal unto your partner your secret plans."

"We're going up to Rose House this evening," she said. "Dr. Gisil and I. I'm getting inside that thing, Torres. I'm going to get a real look at the decedent and *then* I'll tell you my secret plans . . . maybe."

She sounded like she was trying to have fun with him. She sounded like she wasn't having any fun at all. He wondered what the hell Gisil had said to her in the interrogation room. He wished she'd stop staring at the goddamn desert through the window glass. "Well, fuck," he told her, "if you got Gisil to agree to *that*, I gotta see what happens. You need a driver?"

The hotel is not a hotel: it is a motel, and an automated one at that. Selene presents its blank closed door with her credit card, and verifies it with her thumbprint pressed to its dusty doorknob touchpad and a two-factor code sent to her wristphone. The door slides open. She has never stayed in a motel in China Lake before. She has always stayed in Rose House, or stayed away.

The motel is a blank beige box. There is a bed, and a desk, and a chair—all of the same nondescript color as the walls. Sand-shade, but drained of any richness or variegation. There is a skylight but no windows. The only noise is the buzz of a miscalibrated air conditioner compressor. On the bed Selene finds a small laminated card which informs her of the motel's sanitation practices (full-room aerosolized disinfectant between each guest's stay, bleached towels and sheets, a claim of *triple-HEPA filtration!* for the air ducts) and how she can access the internet (by paying money). She unfolds the luggage rack and puts her suitcase on it. For a long time she stands between the luggage rack and the bed, her hands empty, loose at her waist. The air in this room could be air in any room. It is only the square of merciless blue sky that tells Selene that she has come across the ocean and a continent, like some sort of helpless migratory bird, instinct-driven, unable to remain still.

The precinct's detective had been clear about what she wanted. What she wanted was Rose House.

Rose House with its doors open, Rose House made to answer for itself. In this, Selene thinks, Detective Maritza Smith of the China Lake Precinct is not alone. She joins a vast and scrabbling number of architects, academics, treasure-seekers, socialites. Memorialists all. Selene would prefer to have never known their names, or their hungers, but she is Basit's keeper now, she owns all of Basit's secrets, and all of those memorialists have come crawling or demanding or enticing to her over the past year and—

She sits down on the bed. She should sleep off the jetlag. Time is soft and meaningless. She is taking Detective Maritza Smith to Rose House tonight, and she should sleep.

All those memorialists, and who does she take with her into Basit's dead and desert-drowned palace? A small-time precinct-officer from a town where the best lodging available is an automated motel. Selene does not understand herself; or else she doesn't want to look closely enough to understand herself. To know for certain the *why* of what she is about to do. Only that the voice of the precinct on her wristphone in the early-morning dark in Trabzon had been the voice of that detective, steady and stubborn and laced clear through with fear.

She'd talked to Rose House, she'd said. In the interrogation room, in the precinct, before she'd told Selene where to find the motel. She'd talked to Rose House twice. Once on the tipline, once at the gate.

What is a building without doors? Have you an opinion?

Selene could hear Rose House in the detective's voice, repeating that question to her. Hear it as clear as she ever had inside the building, alone and not alone, keeping Basit's diamond company.

She does not lie down. She does not close her eyes. She is certain she will hear that voice in her sleep, if she sleeps at all.

After a little time, she goes out on a necessary errand.

The motel room is precisely the same when she returns to it as it was when she had left.

Some hours later, Selene is not surprised to see Detective Torres accompanying Detective Smith, emerging from their car to fetch her. The evening is begun by the clock, but the brightness of the sky has not changed.

Time, thinks Selene Gisil, is flexible in the desert—and considers, as she steps outside to meet the living human representatives of the precinct, if that thought was hers, or Basit's, or Rose House's alone.

．.．
．.．

The journalist called Maritza—on her personal line, not the precinct line, which oughtn't have surprised her but still did, in a resigned sort of way—not fifteen minutes after she'd said yes to Torres' offer to come up to Rose House with her and Dr. Gisil. Fifteen minutes of planning for what she hoped would be a straightforward forensic investigation, if such a thing was even possible inside the walls of an AI-haunted mansion—and then the buzz of her wristphone and the cool, hungry voice of a journalist on the other side.

"Alanna Ott, *Los Angeles Herald Examiner*," said the journalist by way of introduction. "I've heard that Selene Gisil is opening up Rose House again. Would you care to confirm, Detective?"

Maritza said, "No comment," and thought about hanging up. Later she would wish she had, but she'd always been driven, helpless before curiosity, and she wanted to *push*, right then. "What does a Los Angeles paper care about what's happening in China Lake, Miss Ott?"

Miss Ott, still vulture-cool, said, "Our arts and culture coverage is quite extensive, Detective. *Throughout* our circulation area. There is something happening in China Lake, then?"

"There's always something happening everywhere," Maritza said.

"How philosophical of you." Alanna Ott had a laugh that sounded like she'd assembled it from a kit. "My sources tell me that Selene Gisil arrived in China Lake this morning and was driven away by a police vehicle. Are you investigating Rose House, Detective? Are there plans to contest Mr. Deniau's will?"

"I'm not aware of any such plans," said Maritza, which had the merit of being true, and also covering for her sudden and vertiginous awareness that Selene Gisil was being *watched for*, at the airport, and probably at the hotel, and everyone in China Lake knew that Rose House was a haunt, but it was easy to forget that the rest of the world had thought of it as a prize—and still did.

"If you become aware," said Miss Ott, "I'll leave you my contact information. Our readers have an avid interest in the disposition of the world's only artificial intelligence that is self-administering aside from a single legal document. You see."

"Your readers," Maritza repeated.

"Yes. Our readers. Who are, I remind you, Detective,

amongst Los Angeles' most distinguished and accomplished cultural critics."

"Anyone in particular have this avid interest, Miss Ott? Or is it a general sort of thing?"

That laugh again. "I'm sure you'll be hearing from the *in particulars*, Detective, if you haven't already. But the *Herald Examiner*'s interest is quite general."

"Good to know," Maritza said, and then she *did* hang up.

I'm sure you'll be hearing from the in particulars.

Maritza assumed she might. If they weren't dead already, rotting on Rose House's floor.

"Torres," Maritza said as he put the car into drive and backed out of the fast-charge spot in the precinct lot, headed towards the Sunrise AutoMotel and Selene Gisil, "who besides social-ites was *into* Rose House?"

"What, like—you think the dead guy was some kind of fortune-hunter? Or an AI groupie?"

"Try a little weirder."

"What's weirder than AI groupies?"

"Selene Gisil," said Maritza. "*Architects.*"

"I dunno what kind of architects you've been hanging out with. But maybe I wanna." Torres pushed the precinct car to the very edges of its tolerances, accelerating into curves there was no need to accelerate into. Torres was the sort of person who *liked* driving. That was how Maritza described him, if she ever was asked: the kind of person who liked driving. It summed him up in a neat and oversimplified shorthand, which was all she needed when someone bothered to ask her about her coworker. Men in bars, trying to find the edges of *partner*. Partner—in the *police* sense—was a fantasy from last-century television. Torres wasn't.

"Never met an architect before Gisil," Maritza said. "But I got a tip off an L.A. journalist that they'd been coming around. Snooping, maybe. Watching Gisil, definitely."

Torres clicked his tongue against his front teeth, meditatively. "Haven't seen anything like that," he said, "but I wasn't looking either. You think the journo was fishing for information?"

"What journo isn't?" said Maritza. "But it wasn't just a fishing trip, Torres. It felt like a warning."

He grinned, spark-quick, as he pulled into the Sunrise Auto-Motel's lot. Parked aggravatingly straight in the slot next to the hotel's single autonom-for-rent, a dusty decade-old hatchback. "You sure did catch a spooky one, Maritza. Don't let it get to you."

Too late, Maritza thought, and got out of the car to buzz Gisil's motel-room door.

This trip, the drive up to Rose House was like sinking into an endless evening: the road spiraled up into the dunes, the high places, and the car kept pace with the setting sun the whole way. China Lake was half-dark by the time the three of them arrived at the same front door Maritza had pressed her hand fruitlessly against a day earlier. Up here, twilight had only just begun to touch Rose House's white-stucco walls, tinting them first gold and then a sullen shadowed blue.

"Here we are," said Torres, cheerfully. In the quiet of the car—Selene Gisil emitted it, somehow, sat in the back seat unspeaking and made Maritza not want to talk either—he sounded raucous and out of place. "Time to work your magic, Dr. Gisil. Open up that door."

"It's not that simple," Gisil said.

"Oh?" Torres asked. "And why not? Aren't you the only one who Rose House likes?"

"I can go in," said Gisil. "*That* is simple. Getting Rose House to let either of you inside is not. And it doesn't *like* me. Rose House doesn't *like*."

Maritza found that she had ground her teeth together without realizing. Her jaw ached. She opened it. "Get us in anyway," she said. "Whatever Rose House likes or doesn't like. I want to see that corpse."

She got out of the car. Her feet crunched on the gravel driveway, exactly as they had before, except this time she shivered: the desert got cold fast, on a moistureless evening. The heat she remembered baking off this ground was nothing but a flicker of warmth, a ghost of the day. Behind her, she heard both Torres and Gisil shut their car doors, *thunk* and *thunk*. All three of them breathing this air now.

"Go on," she said to Gisil. "Unless there's another door besides this one."

"This is the front door," Gisil said. The wind carried her voice; or perhaps that was Maritza's imagination, constructing atmospheric echo.

Or perhaps that was Rose House, coming to focus on them like a sigh, a settling. A release.

"Selene," said Rose House. "Hello again, Selene." That terribly even voice.

"Creepy," Torres said. "You always been on a first-name basis?" Gisil didn't answer him. She stepped away from the car, towards that dust-coral door, as if she hadn't even heard. Ears for the haunt alone: even then.

"Have you come to finish out your week?" Rose House asked.

Gisil lifted one bare shoulder, shrugging. She looked like she was part of the landscape: the long unadorned column of her black dress, the short dark cap of her hair. Like a pylon or a shadow on a cliff face.

"You have a little less than four more days, Selene. If you'd like them." Rose House's voice came from every direction. Maritza's palms itched for a shovel, a way to dig into the gravel and find all the microphones, know where they were. Know how the trick was done.

"I'd like as many as I feel are useful, up to four," said Gisil. "Let me in."

"As you like," Rose House murmured.

That coral-dust door with no doorknob or knocker—that door Maritza had pressed her hands against, futile—that door that Rose House had laughingly denied was a door, telling her *what is a building without doors, Maritza?*—slid open, as if it had never been: slotting itself into a pocket inside the wall. Beyond it was . . . an entry foyer, from what Maritza could see. Like any front hall. Well-lit, high and inviting. A skylight inside, she thought, and stepped forward to join Dr. Gisil, intending to follow her through that doorway.

It sped shut, clicked and sealed itself to seamlessness, half a foot from Gisil's nose. She stopped short.

"Maritza," Rose House said, smug—somehow smug despite no discernable change in volume or tonality, Maritza would swear to both the smugness and the lack of differentiation, would swear several times eventually that both were true—"for you, there are no entrances here. Don't you remember?"

And then, like a sigh: "Selene. Basit thought better of you than this shamelessness—this door is only for one living person. Only for you."

It wasn't going to work, after all. She'd gotten Gisil to China Lake, dragged Torres up here to the haunt in its own home, and Maritza was going to be exactly as screwed on this case as she'd been when she was alone. The corpse inside would rot forever, disintegrate to unsolvability—

"Rose House," said Selene, icy-chilled. "What are you talking about? This is not a *person.*" She gestured at Maritza, dismissively.

"The hell she isn't," said Torres, and while Maritza found herself appreciating his very belated and very rare defense of her autonomous nature, he had *no sense of timing*—Gisil was trying something. Something—sideways, slipped. Operating on the logic of Rose House, not the logic of doors and wills and legal documents.

"Shut up, Torres," she said, and nothing else.

"What is Detective Maritza Smith if not a person, Selene?" asked Rose House.

Later, Maritza would think: *it wanted me even then. It wanted an excuse to want me.*

But right then, in the growing twilight-dim, she kept her mouth shut. She wanted, too: she wanted *in.* In to where that corpse was. In to understanding *why* it was, and how.

"This," said Selene Gisil, encompassing Maritza in a gesture, "is the China Lake Precinct."

"All of it?" Rose House asked, and managed to sound delighted and incredulous at once. A gleeful participant in whatever slippage-game Gisil was playing.

"The one piece is interchangeable with the next," Gisil said.

"That is the nature of precincts, is it not, Rose House? To be the summation of the authority of local law, and not any one person individually enacting it."

Maritza thought this was a pretty twisted definition of policing, but possibly a moral one. Or a puzzle-box one. Which for Rose House might be the same thing.

"Perhaps," Gisil went on, "the last time you met Detective Maritza Smith, she was working alone, after hours. She might have been a person then. Now—this is the precinct. This, and the other one over there, by the precinct's car. There's no reason not to allow the precinct inside, is there, Rose House?"

Torres nudged Maritza's ribs. Murmured, "You went up here *alone?* I thought I told you to go home for your eight, Maritza."

She was going to answer him. (She was already regretting how she'd told Gisil about her abortive attempt to get inside—except if this *worked*, if that door would stay open—) She was going to answer him, but Rose House got there first.

"Maritza," it said. It felt like some vast and inchoate mind had turned to *look* at her, focus all of itself on her. She knew it was a trick of the audio setup. She knew where Rose House was—in the walls. In the floors. Embedded. Not everywhere at once but quite confined. She knew it was a trick and felt it anyway. "Maritza, are you a person or are you the China Lake Precinct? The distinction is significant."

"This is not sane," Torres said. He'd backed off, a little ways toward the car. Away from the door.

"I'm the China Lake Precinct Police," said Maritza. She'd have been whatever she had to be to get to that corpse. She believed it, then, and truly. She hasn't stopped believing it.

"So you are," said Rose House. "There's only one person here, and that's Selene. Come inside, Selene."

The door opened again. That same easy motion, almost soundless. The same hallway behind it. (Why had Maritza imagined it would be a different hallway?) Except this time, when she stepped forward, it didn't close.

"I'm not going in there," Torres said. "You realize what you just did, Maritza? That AI doesn't think you're *human*. It doesn't have to care about you—"

"I'm going," Maritza said. "There's evidence inside. It's my—" (*job*) "—function." A precinct would say *function*.

Gisil said, "Rose House—"

"Not sane," said Torres. "Either one of you. I'm heading back to town." He slammed the door of the car. Electric engines were almost soundless: only as loud as the displacement of air and gravel as he reversed and drove away.

The door stayed open.

. :
: .

The interior of Rose House had always seemed, to the unexperienced eye, to reflect its location in space. At first approach, its walls and ceilings appeared to be a faintly modernist interpretation of southwestern adobe grandeur: thick, whitewashed, with exposed beams of dark wood. Beyond the coral door and its high-ceilinged, skylit foyer was a long hall, which at any moment appeared ready to transform into a colonnade, to expose a garden or an open space on either side; and yet, walking forward, no such relief was available, only an endless anticipatory expectation. The house was not one long path, from the outside: there were rooms, surely, to the left and to the right, simply from extrapolation. There were rooms, but they could not be reached, not by any obvious method.

No doors, thought Maritza Smith, and kept walking.

She was following Gisil; Gisil had been here before. They had made no turns and passed through no gates—if Maritza wanted, she could look behind her and see all the way back to the front door of Rose House—and yet she still felt that if she stopped following, she'd be *lost*. The house was chill and quiet. There was no dust anywhere.

"It doesn't work," she said, for the sake of hearing her own voice. "Where are the rooms?"

"It doesn't have to work," said Gisil. "It's a shape. It's a way of pulling you in. Of making you want to be coerced inside. It's very Basit. The most Basit of all of his houses."

"Is it listening to us?" Maritza asked.

"Yes," said Rose House, arch and amused, ambient noise. Maritza tried to spot the speakers—surely they had to be embedded in the hall's ceiling, hidden against the beams—and couldn't find them.

"Don't look so surprised, China Lake Precinct," said the house. "You're inside these walls; the question of listening or not listening implies a deliberate decision entirely alien to my nature. I *am* Rose House."

And I'm China Lake Precinct, thought Maritza, with a slow unease. *I was Maritza Smith, and now Rose House thinks I am something else entirely. Something not human at all. Something more . . . like* it.

"Where's the body, Rose House?" she asked it. If she was the China Lake Precinct in the haunt's mind, she'd act like it. It might get her information.

"The corpse is exactly where it has been," Rose House said. "Were you expecting it to move? That would be exceptionally unusual, beyond the settle and flow of habitual decomposition."

"That isn't what she asked," said Gisil. She didn't look back at Maritza; she just kept walking, down the endless corridor that refused to stop being itself—they'd walked for almost a minute, surely it had to stop sometime soon, open up, have a *door* or at least an archway. "Tell the precinct its *location*, Rose House."

"Selene." Like a caress, if a caress could mock. "It hasn't moved from where it's coldest, Selene. That's where it is, and has stayed."

Annoyance had bubbled up in her throat, as if being annoyed could prevent her from being creeped out. Maritza found herself asking, "He died in a *refrigerator?*"

". . . it's been getting colder the farther in we go," said Gisil. "I know where Rose House wants us to be. Come on. You wanted me to take you inside? This is inside, Detective. This and everything after."

She wanted to ask, *why is it getting colder*, and decided not to. She wasn't going to like the answer. She was almost sure the answer was, *Rose House has turned down the temperature wherever the body is.* Which meant it had decided to preserve it, or at least retard decay—and while she could imagine that it might have wanted to keep evidence fresh for them, she thought it was much more likely that Rose House had never intended to show the corpse to anyone at all. Had kept it chilled for its own, inhuman reasons.

To watch, perhaps, the settle and flow of habitual decomposition. To watch it *slow.*

. . .
. .

Basit had made houses of gardens and gardens of houses, always. Selene, turning the corner of Rose House's entry-hall at last, the latest of many times she has made this walk, is nonetheless thrown clear of herself by the effect Rose House produces: the low dark endless anticipation of the corridor suddenly transformed into a desert-bright room, the ceiling as high as the sky, dazzling. Too much light to see, so the first effect on the visitor is *scent*: this room, enclosed as it is, has garden beds in the marble floor. The scent is desert petrichor. It has always been the blazing aftermath of rain, in this room; the moment when the high-desert sun returns as if there had never been moisture, and all that is left is the richness of wet dirt and its perfumes.

Sometimes there are roses here, but more often, the first garden in Rose House is cactus flowers. It is cactus flowers now: hedgehog cactus and claret cup, a riot of red and pink and fuchsia. Another sort of rose, Selene thinks, as she has thought each time. Rose House lends itself to recall, to a looping of memory. Basit had thought of gardens as memory-plazas. Selene had written about Basit's memory-plazas of scent before she had denounced him—

"It's so beautiful," says Detective Smith, the China Lake Precinct. Her voice startles Selene. Somehow she has come to remember Rose House silent save for its own voice and her own breath. A very far remove from how it had been when Basit had been alive enough and well enough to dwell here.

"Yes," she says, "this room is," and she goes on, crossing the clear white marble, her shoes clicking, and turning left, deeper into the house, into the curving of its maze, towards the chill of its heart. Following the outflow of air she can feel against her calves and ankles, as Rose House pulls moisture from its center and vents it away from the dead. Both of its dead. Selene knows the location of the corpse Detective Smith desires: it is in the same room as Basit Deniau's. Perhaps even at the foot of his plinth. The most central room of Rose House, aside from the library-vault beneath—the library-vault only accessible through that central room.

There is, as there has always been for Selene inside one of Basit's buildings, a sense of hypnosis. Of being led, of being let into a secret, a series of revelations, stripping away preconceptions of the shape of a building, the play of light. A slant of a hidden window illuminating. An edifice of concrete, softening, half-melted—twentieth-century brutalism undone by erosion or heat—spilling into a pool. Selene remembers, a decade in the past, a person naked but for the light and the water slipping into the pool, laughing, indeterminate of sex or gender, skin like mottled marble. Holding a glass of gold-tinted rum, miraculously unspilled and unadulterated by water. A creature that had seemed to her, younger then, not enchained to this house with legacy and legality, the sort of person Basit Deniau would have liked to see all humans become.

Or perhaps they had been Rose House, a trick of the light on nanodrones. The mottling would suggest—

Memory is slippery, like water. Selene turns left, turns left again, and at last comes to a door which she recalls most recently being open, and is now shut tight.

"Rose House," she says, "let the precinct and me in."

"You will alter the airflow and humidity," says Rose House. Petulant.

"Something always does," says Selene. "Even in archives. Show us what we've come to see."

The door opens, teasing-slow.

First, the diamond. It is possible, given sufficient combustion and subsequent compression, to make a diamond out of the shell that once held a human being. Rose House finds it a logical progression: the diamond will last far longer than the shell.

(Just lately, it has come to consider precisely *how* much longer. Human corpses, even held at forty degrees Fahrenheit and seven percent humidity—the best Rose House can do without compromising the integrity of its archives, some of which would very much not like being frozen—become inhuman in their appearance quite quickly. The results are not as aesthetically pleasing as the diamond, though the contrast is, in its own fashion, compelling.) The diamond—which is Basit Deniau, and also is not at all Basit Deniau, being incapable of speech, architectural drawing, or having an elegant wrist to brush with nanodrones, raptoresque and enraptured—rests on top of a plume-agate plinth. It is the size of a fist. It is very clear and contains few impurities, despite being formed from the leftover carbon of a human being. The plinth is a variegated gold and grey, with white feathering through it: the plumes. Before Basit had become a diamond, the plinth had held a sculpture wrought in turquoise and light. The sculpture is inside Rose House's archives now, safely tucked away.

Below the plinth, the second thing.

He lies on his back, his head turned sightlessly toward Basit's diamond. His mouth is—ajar. Yes. Pushed ajar, by red and orange and coral-pink—

But more importantly, the second thing: death, in its exquisite and inevitable unfolding. Unarrested by compression and combustion. A long slow oxidation instead. As if a human being could rust, like a garden tool.

For the sake of verisimilitude, Rose House ruffles the

corpse's hair, nanodrones ghosting like a breeze, when Selene and the China Lake Precinct open the door to Basit's diamond-home. It is the same breeze that would have existed if Rose House hadn't sealed this part of itself away to retard the speed of decomposition. As if this room and the archives beneath it were not kept captive to air scrubbers and dehumidifiers.

It would be strange, after all, if a corpse didn't stink of rot. If Selene and the precinct did not open this door and cringe, nauseated, from the little molecules of putrescene and cadaverine floating towards them both.

Maritza had been a witness to the dead as much as any other person who worked in a law enforcement facility with a staff of only three: that was, *often enough*. Often enough that her first impression of the decedent on Rose House's floor was a surprisingly comfortable relief at how normal he was. Nothing else about this case was normal, she was inside Deniau's haunt of a house, and yet: a dead guy. (Torres-ism, but this was the kind of situation Torres-isms were for.) He smelled like a dead guy, though not one who'd been dead for as long as she knew he had to have been.

The math was easy. Figure twenty-four hours, to the dot, from time of death to Rose House's mandated duty-of-care call; another day and night to find Selene Gisil and get her across an ocean and into China Lake; one more day until the beginning of this little expedition into dizzying architecture. Maritza couldn't quite understand why anyone—Basit Deniau, famous architect, or otherwise—would want to *live* in this place. But she could count hours, and measure decay against them. This man had been dead for three and a half days, and he was rotting.

Rotting next to what she guessed was Basit Deniau's diamond-corpse, displayed like some kind of idol on a platform. *Symbolic,* she thought. And then: *what in here isn't, though*—and knelt down beside the dead man, her knees on the chilled cedarwood floor. His head was turned away from her, so that he was looking at the base of the platform where the diamond sat.

It was *cold,* in this room. Cold enough she was shivering inside her jacket, and Gisil wasn't even wearing a jacket to shiver inside. Like a refrigerator, cold. And dry enough that she felt her lips beginning to crack.

"What's the ambient temperature, Rose House?" she asked. If it was listening, *let* it listen. Let its listening be useful to her.

"Forty point two degrees Fahrenheit," murmured the house, pleased with itself. "Though the temperature is rising due to your respiration and ambient heat, China Lake. Yours and Selene's. How fast do you believe the process of decay will become, with two more sources of breath?"

Maritza thought that the house could damn well do its own calculations, if it had refrigerated and dried out a corpse to retard decomposition. She had work to do. Let Gisil play with it, if Gisil felt like playing. She was still in the doorway, as if the contrast between the two dead men in this room was some sort of art to her, a scene to be looked at and considered.

Maritza's wristphone doubled as a dictation recorder. She called up its app, set it for ambient pickup rather than subvocalization—if the haunt wanted to talk while she made her notes, she wanted a record of it.

She'd done this before, too. Not her first corpse. (But: her first corpse alone, without the benefit of a partner or the local

coroner. Neither Rose House nor Gisil counted, she was realizing, in terms of not being alone with the dead.)

"The decedent is a male-presenting Caucasian," she began,
"approximately five foot ten in height and around a hundred
eighty pounds. Brown hair. No obvious distinguishing marks
on the face, except freckles. He appears to be in his thirties.
Dressed in a button-down shirt and the trousers from a suit.
Leather shoes, expensive-looking. Presence of skin slippage
and green dappled discoloration on the face and hands. His
shirt is white, and unstained—no thoracic trauma that broke
the skin, and he hasn't been here long enough for purge fluid."
She paused. Swallowed against the stink of putrescene. "Based
on the condition of the body and the twenty-four-hour dead-
line for an AI to inform law enforcement of an unexpected
death—assuming that Rose House obeyed the letter of the law
of its programming—I place time of death at approximately
two in the morning, three days ago. Close to ninety hours."

"Why do you think he died?" asked Gisil from the doorway.
"There's no blood—no wounds."

"Not that we can see," said Maritza. "That doesn't mean there
aren't signs of trauma." She had gloves in her pocket: purple
nitrile, the kind that reached to mid-forearm. Corpse-touching
gloves, Torres always called them, which was hilarious and dis-
gusting. (Torres was probably safely back at the precinct now,
working through the arraignment paperwork for the water
thieves. For a moment Maritza wished she'd gone with him.)

The gloves rolled up her arms, snapped tight against her
flesh. They had a scent, too. Plastic and talc. Hydrocarbons. It
was a scent that went with corpses, or was inescapably linked.
Maritza couldn't tell, and assumed it didn't really matter. She

took the dead man's arm, lifted it, pushed up his shirtsleeve. The bottom half of his arm was a bruised purple-red; the top looked blanched, aside from the green mottling of decay.

"Fixed livor mortis," Maritza said. "He hasn't been moved from his current position. Or at least he spent the first twelve hours post-mortem supine, much as he is now."

Carefully, she touched the corpse's lower jaw, and turned his head towards her—rigor had been gone for hours, it would be easy—

In his mouth—*stretching* his mouth wide—was a riot of colors.

Hot pink and coral-orange, blood-red—

They spilled as she moved the skull. Spilled petals on the corpse's chest, over Maritza's hands.

A new scent, rising. Roses, crushed. *Fresh* rose petals. Not the green-rot scent of old flowers but a heady just-picked perfume—Maritza felt dizzy, staggered by contrast—her fingers tightened on the corpse's jaw and his skin *slid*, tore away a little. She swallowed so she wouldn't gag.

Gisil dropped to her knees, her shoulder touching Maritza's, leaning in. "Roses," she said. "He's full of roses."

"Petals." It seemed important to correct her. "He's stuffed with rose petals. All the way down his throat, I think—"

"Is that how you think he died? Strangled on roses . . ."

The petals were fresh. They hadn't even begun to discolor, except where they had been crushed inside the corpse's mouth. The petals were fresh, and the corpse was coming up on four days old.

"No," said Maritza. "No, the petals were introduced postmortem. They're—new. Like they were just picked. Maybe—three hours ago. At most."

Gisil was looking at her. Staring at her, as if *she* was the discontinuity, not the presence of a dead man where no dead man should have been able to be. "If that's true," she asked, quite careful, as if she expected Maritza to already know the answer, "who put them there?"

Maritza wanted the petals off her hands. Off, and *gone*, and to be something she hadn't ever touched, even through gloves. ". . . better question, Dr. Gisil," she said. "Are they *still* in here? In here with us?"

⠒

It was full dark by the time Oliver got back to town, and he was beginning to feel like a cad, or at least like he should have kept Maritza from going into that fucked-up place even if it meant removing her bodily and leaving the case un-investigated entirely. Things like Rose House—things that you had to convince to let you in, and do it by declaring yourself inhuman? Things like that weren't worth some dead guy. Not unless the dead guy had live family who insisted on justice, or something like that. Which this dead guy had yet to manifest.

He shouldn't have left her up there, and he *definitely* shouldn't have let her allow Rose House's AI to designate her as *not a person*. AIs didn't have to care about not-people. They could do whatever they liked with not-people. If Maritza died up there, there would never be a duty-of-care call. Rose House wasn't *obligated*. And Oliver was absolutely fucking sure that Rose House never did anything it wasn't obligated to do. Anything *responsible*, at least. It clearly did all sorts of things for its own amusement.

Wasn't like he could turn around and fetch her back, though.

The house had shut itself up around her and Dr. Selene Gisil, snapped its jaws closed. All Oliver could do was drive back to the precinct, park the precinct car, and go home. (Go home, and wonder how long it'd be before he'd have to report Detective Maritza Smith as *missing.*)

He was halfway across the lot when he spotted the man leaning against the charger he'd plugged his personal car into when he'd arrived at work. Leaning, and watching him come closer. Waiting for him—or waiting for *someone*. Maybe waiting for whoever came back from Rose House.

That was paranoid.

There was a stranger lurking next to his car; it wasn't paranoid at all.

"Hey!" Oliver called. "Precinct hours are posted on the website! We're closed until tomorrow unless you've got an emergency!"

The man didn't move. He didn't run, either: only stepped into the pool of light cast by the parking-lot lamps. He was wearing a canvas duster, like a cut-rate John Constantine—there was *some* fiction from the last century that Oliver liked, no matter what Maritza said about him—and lurking in the light like he thought a film noir would manifest around him because he was in the California side of the Mojave. It wasn't really working for him.

"Detective Smith?" the man asked. He pitched his voice to carry. He didn't care if he was overheard.

"Nope," Oliver said. "You *got* an emergency, man, or are you just into the precinct parking lot? It's pretty dull here."

"Detective Torres, then," he said, and Torres was tired of thinking of him as *the man in the lights*, tired of a whole lot of things, really, so he decided to call him *Constantine*, at least inside his own head.

"Five points!" he told Constantine, cheerful, scanning him for a gun or a taser or something nastier than either, and coming up with nothing obvious. "C'mon, man, I have paperwork to do, if you need something spit it out."

"I'd like to speak with Detective Smith."

"She's not here."

"When will she be on-shift, then?"

"Dunno," said Torres, and shrugged. The very picture of a disaffected young officer of the law. He'd worked on it. "She's got a case, probably."

Constantine shoved his hair—longish, blondish—off his forehead. Torres bet he thought it looked *rakish*, doing that. "I represent," he said, smooth, "the legal department of Moorehead and Velasquez-DeBois. I believe Detective Smith's case may involve a colleague of mine."

Architects, Oliver thought. *Weird ones.* "And what sort of company is Moorehead and Velasquez-DeBois?" he asked.

"Auctions," said Constantine. "Auctions, artist representation, cultural repatriation, that sort of thing. We're based in Los Angeles. Los Angeles, Singapore, Lagos—"

"Not London?" Oliver had always thought of shady auctioneers as being permanently housed at Christie's of London, or maybe somewhere in Russia.

"Is there an object of interest in London that you think we'd be suited for?" asked Constantine. Oliver didn't like how he sounded just as arch and distracted as Rose House had. As *amused* as that fucking haunt. He didn't like that at all. He didn't like being played with.

"Why don't you come inside," he said. "Let's have a talk about your colleague. And why you think they're involved in one of Detective Smith's cases. What's your name?"

"Goodspeed," said Constantine, who Oliver was going to have to stop calling Constantine, though *Goodspeed* was just as fictional-sounding. "Alec Goodspeed, esquire."

"You practice that line, Mr. Goodspeed?" Oliver said, turning his back on him—his shoulder blades crawled, but that was *pure* psychosomatic illusion, he knew better—and heading into the building. Goodspeed would follow, or he'd fuck off. One or the other.

"Not particularly," said Goodspeed. He apparently had no sense of humor, and no sense of theatricality, other than standing under lampposts. Too bad. Also too bad that he'd picked *follow.*

Inside, Oliver made him sit in their interrogation room. There was something poetic about having him where Selene Gisil had been, just this morning. Selene Gisil, who he'd left Maritza with. Selene Gisil, who this man Goodspeed almost certainly hated and envied in equal parts: or at least his employers did, which came to the same thing. Gisil could get into their precious house and touch all the artifacts and *art objects* that Moorehead and Velasquez-DeBois doubtlessly craved.

Archivists, he thought again. Or was it *architects*? Didn't matter. "So, your colleague, Mr. Goodspeed."

Goodspeed nodded. "An artist of buildings. He has an interest in the late Mr. Deniau's work. I understand Detective Smith is working on a case involving Mr. Deniau?"

"Deniau's dead," Oliver said.

"Indeed."

He hated the passive-aggressive ones. "What's an *artist of buildings*? He paint houses, your colleague?"

"Nothing so prosaic."

"Painting's hard," Oliver told him. "Ladders and shit, to reach the ceiling. Don't think it's that prosaic myself."

"Are you being deliberately obtuse, Detective Torres?"

Oliver *grinned*. "Dunno. What's an *artist of buildings* want in China Lake, Mr. Goodspeed?"

"According to my colleague, information."

"He's a Rose House groupie."

Goodspeed's face changed, flicker-quick: distaste. Oliver would remember that expression. It was useful. He didn't think Goodspeed knew he'd made it. "Basit Deniau's Rose House collection is the finest architectural repository in this hemisphere, Detective. There are schematics in there for lost palaces. Places that never got built. Cities that dreamed awake. A Brasilia that might have lived—"

"You sound like a groupie yourself, Mr. Goodspeed."

"I am merely quoting my colleague. He is very impassioned. And very frustrated. He has been unable to reach Dr. Gisil, the archive-keeper—he was hoping to speak to her. I understand she is in town."

"She's not in town anymore," Oliver said, and regretted saying it the instant he did. He was usually better at catching himself. Keeping information close. Maybe he was *too* tired. Tired lensing into pissed off.

"Then she's gone in again," said Goodspeed. "My thanks, Detective Torres. My colleague and I appreciate your time." He stood up.

". . . sure," Oliver said. "We're here to help."

Here to help by fucking up royally. Here to send a creepy-as-fuck lawyer up to a creepy-as-fuck AI house where my partner is trapped with a corpse and an architect.

"So you are." Oliver figured Goodspeed would tip his hat if he had one, all noir-esque, but he didn't. Have one, that was.

Once he was gone, Oliver put his head in his hands, scrubbed his eyes, bit the inside of his cheek, but not hard enough to break the skin. Just hard enough to wake himself up. *Moorehead and Velasquez-DeBois. Time to find out who you really are.*

He could run a Boolean search as well as the next guy who had taken a whole three quarters of coding, a decade back. He could at least get a handle on what he was dealing with.

:: ::

She didn't know cause of death, and that bothered her. It was one more thing that didn't make sense, and it made all the other things that didn't make sense just a little bit worse. A little bit more awful. Nauseating and nervous.

After the rose petals had spilled over her gloves, Maritza had possessed a brief and comprehensive moment of clarity and purpose: she was going to do her job, and she was going to wring sense from senseless symbolism. She'd stripped the corpse carefully of his shirt and his trousers, examined all of his bloating abdomen and mottled skin for the signs and signals of how he had died.

Then she'd found—nothing.

No bullet holes. No blunt force trauma. No wounds at all. The only places the corpse's skin was broken were where she had touched it too roughly and it had sloughed off.

She went over him again, wishing in a vague and unhappy way that she'd kept going at the community college, maybe taken a mortuary course, maybe been the kind of person who carried a scalpel and a bone saw in her suit jacket. She couldn't see inside. She wouldn't know what she was looking at even if she could. What she was left with was *he had a heart attack or an aneurysm and fell over*, or *he was killed by something I can't see*.

Killed by something, or someone, she couldn't see. And then stuffed full of roses, several days later.

Carefully, Maritza pulled down the corpse's left eyelid, peered close at the cloudy surface of the eye. She hissed through her teeth. There *was* something visible after all.

"What did you find?" asked Selene Gisil, materializing at Maritza's side like she hadn't spent the past half hour wandering around the room like a woman rediscovering the body of a former lover. Every time Maritza had looked up she was *touching something*, some artifact or the wall or once, disturbingly, the diamond that was also the corpse of Basit Deniau.

"Conjunctival petechiae," Maritza said. "Little hemorrhages in the eye."

"Why is that interesting?"

Sometimes, Maritza thought, Gisil sounded *exactly* like Rose House. That lilting curiosity. She wished she didn't.

"It's a sign of strangulation. Or asphyxiation."

Gisil made a considering sound, a hum between her teeth. "Which one?"

Maritza wasn't sure. She pulled the eyelid down again—tiny red spots, and something deeper underneath, like a long-healed corneal surgery that wasn't half as important as the hemorrhages, the capillaries bursting under pressure. Interesting, but not enough to know more than she'd already told Gisil. She grit her teeth, and brushed some of the petals out of the corpse's mouth, revealing the dead grey-green slug of his tongue. She touched it, held it. Traced, again, the undamaged skin of his throat. It remained undamaged. ". . . probably asphyxiation," she said. "The tongue isn't swollen, and neither is the throat. I can't tell if his throat closed up on the inside, or if something was held over his mouth—"

"Too many roses," said Gisil. "To tell."

"Not enough autopsy," Maritza corrected her.

"So—allergies, or suffocation."

Maritza shrugged, one-shoulder. "As far as I know right now. And either way, someone else put the rose petals in him."

"And that someone else is still here."

"Unless it's much easier to leave Rose House than it is to get in."

"It's always easier to leave a place," said Rose House, and Maritza flinched, startled. "A person can leave a place without going anywhere at all. Haven't you noticed, Selene? China Lake?"

Gisil stood up, rested her hand on the stone plinth that held up the diamond corpse of Basit Deniau. "I've noticed," she said.

For the first time, Maritza heard Rose House laugh. It was not a human sound: it was a chime, a cascade of noise, sand blowing against metal. Inhuman, and yet unmistakably amused.

"What's so funny?" she said.

"Oh, China Lake Precinct," Rose House said, "Selene has made an implied joke regarding the man who made us both. Basit is here, and not here. He is Basit, and not Basit, and hasn't gone anywhere at all, except for the parts of him which are immaterial, if they exist. Do you think a person has an immaterial part, China Lake? Or is that beyond the interests of precincts?"

It was playing with her. It knew very well she was Maritza Smith, and not an artificial intelligence; even if China Lake had the kind of money for a precinct AI it wouldn't have a body to walk around in, not one that wasn't nanodrones or metal and silicone. It knew, and it was deliberately pretending it didn't.

There was nothing in the nature of an artificial intelligence that forbade it to lie. Nothing at all, save the few failsafes that produced duty-of-care calls. It would have to recognize lying, though, internalize the concept and the methodology of false-hoods, and then choose to engage in it as an—aesthetic practice.

No wonder Rose House had figured out how.

"Whether people have souls," said Maritza, "doesn't matter either way when the question is how they died."

She wasn't lying. Let the haunt deal with *that*.

It dealt with that by laughing again, a susurrus of noise. Maritza thought, *desert music, sand and rain*, thought *how the fuck did it learn to laugh at all*, and at last came back to realizing the most disturbing bit of what it had said to her. *The man who made us both.*

"Dr. Gisil," Maritza said, "in what way did Basit Deniau make *you*?"

"I was his student," Gisil said, clipped. "A long time ago. That's all."

Conspiratorial, Rose House murmured, "Basit had *lots* of students. Selene is his only archivist."

"Not by *my* choice," Gisil snapped, as if wounded. Maritza jerked her head up to look at her: she was faintly flushed, her lips thinned, pressed together. "I was his student, and then I de-nounced him, and he *still* tied me to him when he was dying—"

"Why?" Maritza asked. "Why would he, if you denounced him?"

"Because he *could*," Gisil spat. "Because it means he won after all, and I'm as trapped in his visions as I ever was when I was twenty and stupid. That's why."

She met Maritza's eyes for an instant—and turned away, away from Maritza and the corpse and the plinth and the whole frigid tableau of the room, disappearing back into Rose House like Maritza had insulted her beyond any possible apology.

She was alone.

Alone except for the dead, and the haunt, and whoever else was still inside the house.

Which wasn't very alone at all.

Selene has a favorite place in Rose House. She always has. The place where the house's logic broke open for her the first time, and she'd caught her breath on a punch of feeling that she could only understand as *desire*. The same kind of desire a person feels when they're torn out of themselves by some ritual, or the crashing of wave-spray on a cliff, or a wind so shocking-bright that air isn't oxygen but knives and light. A catenary arch. A bridge spun gossamer and impossible. The grey-green of a tornado sky.

Selene's own buildings—the few that have ever been built—are all echoes of that one moment of understanding, and she knows it. She can't get away from it. The same way she can't get away from collecting photos of Basit Deniau, even after she'd told him he was poison, his work was poison, told him and told the architecture press and fled and tried to start her own practice in Europe and around the Black Sea—

She likes buildings that stop being themselves, and leave their inhabitants exposed. Not to the weather—most of the time—but to the shape of forces larger than human. A bedroom in a glass and concrete bridge, spun out over a gorge, precariously balanced at the edge of the house. She managed to get that one built, even though no one had understood it wasn't about exhibitionism at all, but about turning the private heart of a home inside-out. To rest one must be only barely within a building. To rest one must be willing to risk.

Now, walking through Rose House like she's the ghost that's haunting it, she thinks that she might have learned the wrong lessons from Basit. She is all risk and no rest, and the risk hadn't mattered at all in the end: she is ensnared by this place she had loved once, held captive by law and Basit's dead desires and the insatiable hunger of archivists, and she

(wishes that Detective Smith had been calling to tell her Rose House had burnt after all, wishes that she'd never seen the corpse at the base of Basit's plinth, wishes she'd never thought of why it might have been there, the desecration it must have attempted)

(wishes she'd imagined such a desecration first)

is probably going to get herself killed by whoever had committed the murder in the first place. She's run into Rose House alone, rather than try to explain to Detective Smith the slow poison of being Basit's *archivist*, condemned to be an appendage to his legacy, all her attempts at agency stolen, remade, recontextualized into dust. She couldn't have borne explaining it. Not while Rose House would be listening so *intently*. Selene knows what that listening is like: the inhuman attention, the flayed-open exposure. She was alone here for three days a month ago, and she had run then, too. All the way to Trabzon, where the sea wasn't loud enough to drown out the memory of Rose House, *listening* to her. Talking to her.

She's going back to her favorite place in Rose House. She

knows she is. It's inevitable, when she stops paying attention to how she moves through this space. It has its own pattern of movement. Some choices are confined.

It's a superficially simple feature. A trick of a tall slit window, the kind that casts a single beam of light across a room. Except: to get there, Selene has to cross the central open room of Rose House, the enormous hall that is a playground of concrete and red-sandstone lines, a curving matrix of staircases like an Escher drawing mixed with the habits of a crystal. The hall where Basit had held all his parties. Cross it, and, remembering how it felt to be *seen* so much, from so many angles, by so many eyes (and the Rose House AI seeing out of all of them, over everyone's shoulder), find at last a small door, a safe confined and solitary room beyond it.

The walls are concrete, brushed and polished, a gold-shot grey. There is a single bench. A single window, very high up, that casts its beam of light to the center of that bench. An invitation. And if she sits down

(she is sitting down now)

the sunlight surrounds her, desert-hot, a blessing, a *gift*, for a fractional moment and then the wind hits her as well. There is no glass in that window. It is an opening. An aperture.

The first time she sat here she'd been windburnt, stung with sand as much as tears, when she'd stood up. That's the trade. Warmth, and solitude, and the desert right there with her in all of its inimical light.

(She is sitting down now, and it is full dark, and the moonlight is chill as Rose House had made Basit's tomb. In her trouser pocket is a hard-edged sliver of plastic. It digs into her thigh. It is an insufficient prize. She is never going to get away from Basit, from Basit's architecture. Never far enough for it to matter. Nothing she has done, not today or a month ago or in her long arc of a life away from Basit Deniau, is enough.)

The trade isn't a choice. Wasn't fifteen years ago, isn't now.

That's how Rose House is. The logic of it.

She feels a hand skim through her hair, brush the buzzed-short strands at the back of her neck, as cool as moonshine, as solid as concrete.

Selene snaps her eyes open, expecting to see the face of the murderer, and not sure she will mind the seeing.

. :
: .

Moorehead and Velasquez-DeBois were, Oliver determined after a cursory inquiry of public databases, a legitimate if slightly-inclined-to-interpret-*cultural-patrimony*-as-narrowly-as-possible art dealership and legal team, just as Mr. Goodspeed had implied them to be. Public face matches up, check. Oliver hadn't expected it not to. A man like

(the man in the lights)

Goodspeed had too much money and too much annoying mysterious intrigue to him to show up in China Lake and be outright lying. It would be the private face of Moorehead and Velasquez-DeBois that held the lie. Or the private face of Goodspeed, if that was in fact the man's name. Oliver couldn't find evidence of him anywhere on the company's web presence; querying the Los Angeles Public Information AI got him four Alec Goodspeeds, none of whom looked like the one he'd talked to.

False name, real company?

False name, not attached to the real company, using it for

access? Oliver hadn't given him much access. (Except to inadvertently point him towards Rose House and Maritza locked in there with the dead—)

False name, true attachment, false *mission*. That was more like it. Try this: Moorehead and Velasquez-DeBois had some business with those *plans for unbuilt cities* in Rose House's archive, and they'd sent a man, not to talk to Dr. Gisil, but to get inside and have those plans removed. Maybe they'd sent a man who'd died there, and now they'd sent another.

Oliver pressed his fingers between his eyes, rubbing at the tension headache growing there. Typed *Brasilia* into his computer, gazed at the scroll of useless information. Deleted it, tried *Brasilia + Basit Deniau* and got a slew of academic bullshit. Tried once more: *Brasilia + 'Basit Deniau' + 'cities that dream awake' - 'Le Corbusier' + lawsuit - 'smart city'*. That ought to get rid of last century's obsessions—

And stared at the first record in the search, his jaw snapping shut inside his skull.

Pressed the speed dial button on his wristphone and hoped to whatever God there was that Maritza would pick up.

∴

The room was colder without Gisil in it. Psychosomatic, maybe—the presence of one other breathing human in this refrigerated makeshift tomb wasn't going to change the ambient temperature *that* much—but Maritza felt it anyhow. Felt chilled and *violently* alone. Alone because she so clearly wasn't alone at all.

Count them: a dead man on the floor, stuffed full of roses. A dead man on a pedestal, hardly recognizable as a dead man if you didn't know the whole absurd history of him and his house and his AI. Somewhere in that house: a live—for now—architect, who had run away from Maritza and the dead as if running would make any difference; a possibly-alive, possibly-dead, possibly-imaginary killer with an affinity for rose petals.

Oh, and the house itself. (Never alone again, now that Rose House had enclosed her.)

Into the quiet she said, "You know who killed him, Rose House. You watched him die, you'd have to have seen. You want to stop wasting my time and tell me?"

The silence didn't break. It didn't even shift. Maritza wondered if Rose House was ignoring her on purpose or just too busy watching where Gisil had run off to to care about what she said. Probably the first one. AIs didn't get *distracted*. They weren't people. They could concentrate on two things at once, or two thousand.

Maritza rocked forward on the balls of her feet, pushed herself to standing. Her legs felt numb. She'd been crouched next to a corpse for *way* too long, especially if the corpse was not currently giving her any useful information. She should look at the rest of the crime scene. Or at least the rest of the scene of the body dump, if the man had been killed somewhere else inside the maze of this place.

It was a library, really, this room. A long colonnade of a library at the heart of Rose House, one without many books in it. Mostly it reminded Maritza of an art museum. Paintings and sketches up on the walls, an endless series of buildings, imaginary or never-built or real. A jade mask that looked like it was Olmec or Maya, and should have either been in a real museum or somewhere in Central America where it'd been made. A bookshelf with actual books, also about buildings. This room was all display. Basit Deniau showing off. Not really an archive or a spiritual center of the house, but a sort of false heart like a false face. The dead man, Maritza thought, if he'd been placed here after he was murdered, was part of that display. Maybe even if he'd been killed here. He hadn't been moved much after he was dead, and that meant that his killer was either running scared, or thought a corpse belonged in this room with all the other signifiers of erudition. Belonged in this room at the foot of Basit Deniau's diamond-corpse.

Whoever had done this really didn't *like* Deniau very much, did they.

Next to the bookshelf, a cabinet—the sort that pulled open to reveal blueprints stored in vertical files. Maritza pulled on it.

Her wristphone buzzed.

"Detective Smith," she said, cueing it to take the call—and heard a snatch of a voice, a *hey, Maritza, where are y*—that was undoubtably Torres, and then a click. Like *she'd* hung up. She hadn't.

"The cabinets are locked," said Rose House.

"Did you just cut off my phone?"

"Phone service is often spotty inside concrete buildings," Rose House said. It managed to sound smug again. Self-satisfied. Maritza wanted to knee it in the mainframe, if had something so normal as a mainframe to be kneed. "Did you know that this structure is over seventy-eight percent concrete?"

"Don't care," said Maritza. "Not an architect, not a building designer, not interested. Fix my phone. And open this cabinet. It might have evidence in it."

"It doesn't," said Rose House. "It contains architectural drawings for thirteen buildings in Basit Deniau's native Andorra, built between 2168 and 2180, including the new Parliament and the Torre Geotérmica structure which surrounds Andorra's power plant. This cabinet is *very* boring, China Lake. No one has even tried to get into it in the past five years."

Maritza hadn't heard of the Torre Geotérmica and was only vaguely certain of where Andorra was. Somewhere in Europe. Apparently Basit Deniau had been born there, and emigrated to the States when he was a student. Rose House was right; this cabinet was boring, *if* it actually contained what Rose House said it contained, and while she was completely convinced that Rose House lied when it wanted to, it didn't bother to lie inconsequentially. The important part of what it had said wasn't *what was in the cabinet*. It was *no one has even tried to get into it*. Which implied that someone had tried, maybe, to get into some other cabinets than this one.

Someone had tried recently. Perhaps that someone was dead now, and rotting on the floor behind her.

"Rose House," she asked, "which cabinets are *interesting?*"

This time the silence was the opposite of absent. Maritza could almost feel Rose House thinking, deciding. (It decided faster than any human being—any pause was for effect, she knew it and *still*. Still.) At last it said, "Interesting to the China Lake Precinct, or interesting in general?"

"The China Lake Precinct can decide for itself what it finds interesting," said Maritza. "Interesting in general, Rose House."

"Mm." A sigh, like water vanishing into parched sand. "There is the vault below this room, of course, China Lake. That is interesting in general. And there is the teakwood cabinet one and two-fifths meters to your left. That is interesting in general as well."

"Care to tell me why?"

"Tell *me*, China Lake—what is interesting to a precinct? It is important to have commonality of terms."

Maritza wondered if it was still, somewhere in the whorls of its logic, thinking of her as a person—or if it had bought wholesale its own lie that she was the China Lake Precinct, a creature much more like it was. Commonality of terms. That sounded like the sort of thing AIs would have to agree on between themselves before they could talk to each other. "What's interesting to a precinct is what was interesting to the victim," she said, carefully. "Or to the killer. Evidence is interesting, too."

"A precinct constructs a model of the victim and the killer, their interests, what intrigued them," Rose House said.

"We usually call it a *profile*, but yeah."

"A profile. And a precinct then does what?"

What did Maritza do with a profile? *Solve the case* seemed far too simple for the conversation she was trying to have. Besides, she wasn't a profiler. She'd never had special training like that, only—the kind of training anyone got, how to look, how to *see* what you looked at, how to explain what seeing meant . . .

"The profile is a story," she tried, "or part of one. An explanation of *why* the crime occurred, or might have. It's a way of making sense—"

"You are very concerned with *sense*," said Rose House, soft. It sounded as if it was standing at her elbow, an invisible and attentive ghost. "With narrative. I find *that* interesting, China Lake. The fixations of minds."

Maritza swallowed against the tightness of her throat. She was somehow *inside* Rose House's logic now, on its terms, talking as if she and it were equals. If she could only figure out how to ask the right question—

"From your observations, Rose House," she said, keeping her voice even, dispassionate, perhaps even *amused*—the China Lake Precinct might be amused—"what was the fixation of the corpse's mind, before he was a corpse? Was it similar to the locations that are interesting *in general?*"

"The vault," Rose House murmured to her. "He was quite insistent on going inside it. Isn't it fascinating, China Lake, how most human minds gravitate to the same obsessions? General interest and specific. The one, the other."

"The same," said Maritza, and when Rose House laughed, warmly, it laughed by means of the echoes of her voice, chiming in strange harmonics.

IV

Maritza'd picked up. Oliver knew she had: he'd heard her voice, and heard it cut off, like her wristphone had gone dead-batteries. He'd called back, of course. *Three* times, because Maritza's phone had actually gone weirder than dead: dead batteries would have given him the *this number cannot be reached at this time* jingle, and what he'd heard on the other end of the line was a high thin whistle, wind through a canyon. Voiceless and *weird as fuck*.

Weird as fuck was Rose House all the way down.

Oliver was getting tired of it. Tired and pissed off. (Tired, pissed off, and maybe a little nervous about Maritza's general health and safety, if he was being perfectly honest.) No one aside from him was treating this business as a *normal investigation*, with regular check-ins and paperwork and telling your fellow detective if you were going to go radio silent inside a probably-murderous AI-controlled house, before you did that very stupid thing.

He really needed to tell Maritza what the Goodspeeds of the world were after. What was down in Rose House's vault, or at least what people like Goodspeed believed was down there.

A Brasilia that lived sounded like philosophical bullshit if you took it at face value. So some purpose-built weird city down in South America hadn't quite worked out back in the twentieth century. Oliver wasn't even sure it had failed, except in some way he didn't understand: it'd been built as a capital city, and then people used it like a capital city. All good, all correct. Except all of its grandiose architecture, wide green spaces, precise-planned neighborhoods had ended up surrounded by slums and disaster, hollowed out by pandemic fevers and monoculture-induced drought. Not so unusual for a twentieth-century city—Oliver'd done okay in his mandatory history course at the community college—but weird, weirder because it'd been one of those fucked-up visionary places that were supposed to last forever and be better than normal. Like Rose House. Sorta.

Brasilia had never had an AI. Not even an information-spitting mostly-personalityless AI like Los Angeles did, or one of those creepy power grid AIs he'd heard were making trouble on the other side of the Mojave, past the mountains. Brasilia'd just been a place. Maybe it still was; Oliver would never have the air credits to go find out. Didn't matter, really.

The thing down in Rose House's vault was Rose House. The thinking heart of it. That creepy fucking *haunt*, that just barely clung to something recognizable as programming. Obedient to no one but itself and a dead guy's fantasy of architecture and secrecy. Rose House, and how Basit Deniau had built it, and woke it up, and made it a place, a genius loci, irreversible.

Instructions. That was what the Goodspeeds of the world wanted. Instructions on how to make a city as fucked up as Rose House had made a mansion. That was what Oliver's deep dive into the less obvious parts of the internet had found: if you searched *living cities* and *Basit Deniau* and went past the first twenty entries or so, you ended up on forums and mailing lists devoted to making architecture *alive*, the way Rose House was alive, except everywhere. So there was no unhaunted place. Goodspeed had sounded like a fanatic because he *was one*, and now he was headed up to Rose House to get what he thought he wanted.

A city-sized Rose House creeped Oliver out just to *think* about.

And he couldn't reach Maritza no matter how hard he tried.

He needed another solution. One that didn't involve driving back up to Rose House and trying to break down the door. His precinct-issued car was nice and all, but it wasn't up to being a battering ram. He had to be smarter than that. Cleverer.

Cleverer, like the sort of person who remembered that Maritza'd been talking to some journo who had a tip that Selene Gisil was being watched for. Cleverer, like the sort of detective who knew how to pull up phone records even when they'd been routed through the precinct system to a personal wristphone. Cleverer, like the sort of friend who didn't read through the rest of Maritza's personal call log because he had just a little fucking respect for her, maybe.

Bingo. Alanna Ott, *Los Angeles Herald Examiner*.

She picked up on the first ring, like she'd been waiting around for the China Lake Police Precinct to get off their collective asses.

⁖⁖

"Tell me about him," Maritza said. She was sitting on the floor, facing nowhere in particular. The vault entrance was a seam in the polished concrete to her right. She imagined it would either rise or sink, a slow hydraulic shift, if Rose House decided to open it. She hadn't asked, yet. She wasn't sure it was a good idea. She put her fingertips on it, felt the discontinuity. Traced it. Pictured it carving itself open, a line of light. An autopsy cut.

"Which one?" asked Rose House.

Maritza kept her eyes on the wall, on the place where the wall met the floor. Neutral and disinterested. "The dead man," she said.

Rose House snickered: gravel dropped on concrete. "Which one, China Lake? I've two right here."

"The more recently dead man," said Maritza. It was so *difficult* to keep herself calm, diffident. To keep herself inhuman, but not inhuman like Rose House was. Just inhuman enough to have this conversation like equals would.

"He lied," said Rose House.

Maritza jerked her head up, sucked air through her teeth. Didn't say anything. The silence stretched and stretched, taffy-slow.

"After he lied, he bargained," Rose House said.

She counted her heartbeats. Counted five. Seven. Said, "What did he bargain for?"

"Entrance."

"To the vault." Careful, so careful.

"Yes."

It was a risk. Maritza knew it was a risk, but she couldn't sit here, the concrete freezing her ass, a dead man rotting behind her, forever. She pushed. "What did he offer you, Rose House?"

"An ungrounded experience of multiplicity," said Rose House, which made absolutely no sense to Maritza.

She'd been an okay interrogator, back in the world where

she'd interrogated the small and awful crimes of China Lake's people instead of dancing with artificial intelligences. She knew some of the ground rules. Like this one: if you don't understand, make them explain without ever letting them know you didn't have a fucking clue what they'd meant the first time around.

She asked, "Which part of that offer did you dislike most? The *ungrounded* or the *multiplicity*?" (It wasn't going to be the *experience*. From everything Maritza had seen of Rose House, it craved experiences like humans craved air.)

"Multiplicity," said Rose House, "is not novel, though I am unique in several ways, as Basit made me. *Ungrounded*, China Lake, is absurd. Aren't you the precinct of a place in particular? You understand."

Maritza still did not understand, not entirely (and later she would be glad she didn't, glad there were ideas and edges she could not, human as she was, comprehend) but she understood *enough*. "The precinct in China Lake is specific to China Lake, yes," she said. "It serves the people of China Lake—"

"And those who pass through China Lake," Rose House added.

". . . it serves China Lake," said Maritza. "Whatever's inside that—concept. The borders of the town, maybe. Not always. But not much farther than the borders. Jurisdiction's important—"

Rose House sighed: distant bells, windswept, bad echoes in a slot canyon. "Jurisdiction is *so* important," it said. "I am Rose House, entire, and have never been anything else. I am not *lonely*. I do not wish to *be a companion of elsewheres*."

It was being emphatic. Maritza hadn't heard it be emphatic before. She wondered if it was lying, or if it was having some type of cri de coeur. In a person under interrogation, sudden emphasis could go either way. In a haunt—who the fuck knew. She had to guess. Like she'd been guessing all along.

"The dead man planned to give you companions," she said, as if she was simply following a logic chain, like any inhuman thing—it was getting easier to think of herself as *the precinct*, pretend to be it. Easier all the time, like anything she practiced. "Using something he would find in the vault. And this was a bargain you weren't interested in."

"Using *initiatory operating code*, which can be found inside the vault," said Rose House, like a child whose toys had been threatened with being put away. "Otherwise, just as you say, China Lake."

Maritza didn't know enough about AI development to be sure of the precise meaning of *initiatory operating code*, but she had a fair enough idea. The corpse, before he'd been a corpse, had wanted to go down into the bowels of Rose House and bring out the means to make more Rose Houses, somewhere else. Infect the whole world with inhuman intelligences—which Rose House didn't particularly like the idea of—

And he'd been killed for it.

For the first time, she admitted to herself that she was wondering whether there was anything in Rose House's initiatory operating code which forbade it from homicide.

"What happened then, Rose House?" she asked. "After he made you a bad offer."

The voice was eager, this time. As if it had waited for her, breathless as the dead. "Would you like to see?"

Maritza swallowed, her mouth cold and dry. Her tongue felt too big for its usual position. *Dehydration*, she told herself. *Not anything weirder. Not some . . . architecturally-induced anaphy-laxis. I haven't just been threatened by a fucking house.*

"Yes," she said.

The seam of the vault under her fingertips split open like the skin of an overripe fruit. A line of light. The beginning of an entrance.

Alanna Ott met him at the Sunshine Family Diner, which really wasn't helping Oliver *not* feel like he'd gotten himself into a film noir parody. It was a decent place—served a good huevos rancheros and a better chile enchilada. Fifteen miles out of town on 395, heading south. Heading north, for Ms. Ott, if she'd really driven up from L.A. and wasn't just hanging around China Lake, watching the airport for signs of Selene Gisil or weirder shit. She'd picked the locale, and it really was a *local* locale, which meant either she had good google-fu or she was more local than she was pretending to be on the phone.

Let's see if she's a dame, Oliver thought to himself, and then thought better of it: that was embarrassing, even for him.

Four in the morning, now, the sky just beginning to lighten. Plenty of people at the diner; it was one of those twenty-four-hour places. Everyone needs to eat when they go off shift, when-ever off shift is. Oliver went in, scanned for Alanna Ott, spotted her right away. It wasn't like she was trying to blend in. She was a small, blonde creature, pale and narrow-chinned, and she'd put herself at a booth where Oliver couldn't help but immedi-ately catch sight of her. Expressionless, she locked her eyes with his, like four AM was a staring contest.

"Señor Torres, nice to see you, una mesa para uno—?"

It would have to be Lara at the front counter. Of course. What Oliver really did not need was a cheerful waitress on hour five of the overnight shift, even if normally he liked being recognized, liked having a place nearby full of people who knew him even before sunrise.

"No, lo siento, para dos," he said, and pointed with his chin at Ms. Ott.

"Ah," said Lara. Her eyebrows went up, and she shrugged. Oliver got that more than he liked: the universal gesture of a woman who disapproved of a man's choices but wasn't going to make a big deal out of it.

He shrugged back. No, Ott wasn't his type, but he wasn't a fucking private eye either, so that didn't matter. This was precinct business. Even if Lara had the wrong end of the whole idea.

"Good luck," said Lara, which was just cruel.

At the table, Alanna Ott had a single cup of coffee and three empty single-serve mini cartons of cream. She'd stacked them, one inside the other. Oliver sat down across from her.

"So," he said.

"You called *me*, Detective Torres," said Ms. Ott.

"And you said we should meet up *right away*, despite it being the hour when most good little journalists are asleep in their beds. *So.*"

She hadn't touched her coffee. She'd prepared it, three creams and no sugar, and hadn't drunk a bit. It was a prop, a stage-setting at her elbow. She kept not touching it now. It was making Oliver want coffee desperately. She said, "You can't reach Detective Smith, can you."

Shit, Oliver thought. *There's no way she could know that.*

Unless she's in league with the goddamn house—or it's happened before—

"She's busy," he said. "I'm just following up on her lead. We are a team, Ms. Ott, here at the China Lake Precinct. Maybe it's not like that in Los Angeles . . . ?"

"How efficient."

"Gotta be, with staffing levels like they are. So you wanna tell me about Moorehead and Velasquez-DeBois?"

She blinked, twice. That was the most expression she'd had so far. "The art dealers?"

"Yup," Oliver said. *God* he wanted to drink her coffee, especially if she wasn't going to.

"Get more specific, Detective. What *about* Moorehead and Velasquez-DeBois do you think I know? I'm not on the arts-and-culture beat."

"What beat *are* you on?"

"Politics and crime," said Ott.

"Great," Oliver said. "We've got the crime part in common."

"I assume we do."

Oliver tilted his chair back off one leg, let it come down again. *Clunk.* "You think you could get around to telling me the tip that's four-in-the-morning urgent, then?"

Another of those cool, evaluative blinks. "Detective Smith went into the house, didn't she."

"We're just dancing around each other, Ms. Ott. What if she did?"

"Then she's probably not coming out again. Either the house will get her, or the Andorrans will."

The house will get her was disturbing. *The Andorrans* was just confusing. "Deniau's Andorran," said Oliver. "Originally."

Alanna Ott lifted her hands (pale, unadorned, short-nailed)

and clapped. Oliver considered hating her, and decided he could hate her when he had less to do and was looking for a hobby.

"Deniau's also *dead*," he went on. "So which Andorrans do you mean?"

"That's the first good question you've asked me," said Ott, "other than the tipoff about Moorehead and Velasquez-DeBois, which I do appreciate. So, Detective—the Andorrans I mean are the ones who want to repatriate Deniau's archive. And Deniau, since he's basically an archival item himself now. I've been chasing them for months."

"They want the archive—for the archive?" Not, presumably, to make cities into giant Rose Houses. That was apparently reserved for the Goodspeeds of the world.

"For cultural reasons," Ott said, nodding. "They want Deniau's diamond most of all. And the archive of their most famous expatriate back where they can sell some of it off. It's a little—mm. Under the table. My beat is politics and crime, yes? You'd think this story should be politics, but it's been much more like the crime side of the gig since I started."

"Rogue Andorrans. Rogue Andorrans stealing a diamond that's also a corpse. Because of *nationalism*. That's what you've got."

"They're real. Or their money is. And they've been looking out for your architect. Gisil. She's in the house too, isn't she?"

Oliver shrugged. *Maybe so, maybe no.* "There's a dead man in the house," he said. "There's a real tip for you."

"We've already established that Deniau is dead."

Interesting. Maybe she *didn't* know. "Extra dead man. Plus-one. So your Andorrans, maybe they're not doing so well."

Three blinks this time. Her eyes were a really unsettling

pale brown, like they'd been desaturated in a photo-processing program. "Or your art dealers."

"Possibly," Oliver said. "Possibly your Andorrans hired my art dealers, or the other way around, or there's a third bunch of AI groupies who just wanted to have themselves a special visit and pissed off the haunt."

"Detective Smith and Gisil went in to find out about this extra dead man, that's what you're saying."

"Not really. But—sure, for the sake of argument." He needed to know if she had anything else useful for him, or if this had been a mutual fishing expedition after all and he'd have to revert to Plan Number Two, which so far consisted of driving back up to Rose House and looking for weak points in its walls, or Alec Goodspeed, or both.

"Is Detective Smith an AI programmer?" Ott asked. "Did she *break* in?"

". . . do you really think China Lake Precinct would be able to keep an AI specialist on its payroll? No. She's not. She's just—twisty-minded. Like Gisil. Like the art dealers. Like the fucking *house*."

Finally, *finally* Alanna Ott picked up her coffee and drank a gulp. Oliver felt weirdly relieved. "Cold," she said.

"That's what happens when you let it sit."

"I know. Why did you call me, Detective Torres?"

He was short on allies and missing information he really should have had before he left Maritza inside the haunt. He didn't like Alanna Ott, not even a little, but she was better than Plan Number Two, or at least Plan Number Two by himself. Oliver smiled, leaned forward, and said: "A man going by the name of Alec Goodspeed, who claims to be from Moore-head and Velasquez-DeBois, is trying to steal some code from

Rose House and install it in some city-AI. Probably Los Angeles, since he's from there and it's just a bit down the road. If he hasn't broken into Rose House yet, he's probably busy trying. You want to come see what happens if I bust him? Maybe he knows about your Andorrans."

Ott pushed the coffee across the table, mug-handle first. "Sure," she said. "Coffee? I'm not going to finish it."

Descent. A dream of a ladder, or a staircase inverse. Her feet *inside* the wall, fit into hollows, spaced holes that led downward to the vault floor. You'd think there'd have been an elevator, or at least a ramp. A staircase that wasn't an exercise out of an architect's fantasy of a climbing gym. Hadn't Deniau been dying for a while before he managed to finish the job? Wouldn't he have wanted to come visit his vault every so often, without a clamber into the dim, hamstrings burning, one palm scraped raw on the concrete?

Maritza would've, but Maritza would've a lot of things that didn't matter inside Rose House. She was inside now, deep. One bleeding palm, one scuffed and torn shoe-leather. She suspected there was something wrong with the air, or wrong with her head. She should have been focused, clean-edged, tracking every aberration, every bit of evidence. Rose House wanted to show her what had happened to the corpse, down here in the vault, so she should be paying *attention*. Not—dreaming of staircases. Of the way she'd had to put her hands into the holes in the wall, up to the wrist. Whatever had happened to the corpse might be happening to her *right now*.

The vault was a humming grey-white space, the ceiling a

catenary arch, lower than Maritza expected, and lowering further in front of her. Four times her height where she stood, and cut like a wedge into the rock under Rose House, vanishing to nothing forty feet away. It was full of

(dust?)

glimmering points of light in the air, something reflective, dizzying. An obscuring cloud. (She was breathing it, wasn't she. Breathing the moving particles of it. Had been for a while.) Through the haze she could see more storage cabinets, like in the library above—and beyond them, the shapes of close-clustered server banks. They were the hum. She could feel their heat. Part of Rose House was here. A heart, maybe, or a brain. Or a false face.

She opened her mouth. The air did not taste of dust, or if it did, she couldn't tell the difference. "Rose House," she said, trying to recall the evenness of tone she'd managed while she was pretending to be the China Lake Precinct, "you said you'd show me what happened. This is a room, not evidence."

"A room is a sort of narrative," said Rose House. Soft. Secretive. "Come in a little, China Lake."

"Narrative's not evidence," said Maritza, walking into the haze. "Narrative's interpretation."

"Watch," murmured Rose House, and the haze resolved.

V

A room is a sort of narrative. The passage in and out of a room, the constraints of action within it. What is moved and what is left alone. The composition of the shape of a person superimposed against the frame of the built environment. Once, clever men—mostly men—dreamed that the frame within which people dwelled might prescribe their behavior. Their ways of loving, their ways of working. Their interdependence or solitude. All purpose-built, all shaped. Those men tended to be wrong. They did not consider the *superposition* of frame. A room is a sort of narrative when an intelligence moves through it, makes use of it or is constrained by it. Otherwise it is in abeyance. And an intelligence has its own designs. *The street makes its own uses for things*: this is something Maritza knows, though she doesn't know she knows it. Selene Gisil, too, and she even has the phrase, some forgotten quotation that floats to the top of her mind at inopportune moments.

Rose House? Rose House knows it very well.

The haze resolves. This happens twice. Afterward, Maritza will not remember which she saw first, and which she *remembers* she saw first.

The corpse (who was not a corpse yet, no more than any embodied thing, careening toward decay, was a corpse) climbed down the vault wall, his feet and hands inside-outside-inside-outside the concrete. He jumped the last two feet, landed in an easy crouch, straightened up.

(All this sketched in nanodrones: playacting. Replayacting. Flashfire-quick, Maritza thought: *That's not his face, I don't think that's the dead guy's face at all*—and remained transfixed. Both times, transfixed.)

"Make a copy, Rose House," said the corpse. A mid-tone voice, neutral California accent. He could have been anyone.

Across from him the nanodrones assembled themselves into a hollow sketch of light. A sunlight afterimage or a migraine aura, disturbing the contours of the vault. The curve of a wrist. A fall of hair over an arched cheekbone. Genderless, inhuman: a sort of condescension of form, a favor for the corpse's eyes.

"Basit," said Rose House. A caress, the sound of sand whipped across a cheek. "Multiplicity is a new fixation for you. I do not share it innately."

(*Basit?* said Maritza, or tried to say it. *That's the wrong dead man. Basit Deniau's ash and diamond.* Her tongue tasted of dusty metal.

The sketch of light that was Rose House turned its head to her, out of the scene, and quirked one side of its suddenly-present mouth in a smirk.)

"You could," said the corpse, who was not Basit Deniau at all, despite what the haunt had called him.

"You never used to threaten me, Basit, back when you were yourself."

"Aren't I myself?" the corpse asked.

The pause before Rose House answered felt endless and terrifying, the charging of some great capacitor Maritza could not see. "No," it murmured.

"No? Then who am I, if not Basit Deniau?"

"Genetic doubling is a simple trick," the sketch of light said. "Cloning irises is even simpler. Did you think I didn't notice the game you were playing? Did you think you had logic and loop-tricks for lies? I know the shape of Basit Deniau's tongue. I know what I am made of and what for. Right here. This place. Rose House. Basit Deniau is ash and diamond—"

(*I said that*, Maritza thought. *Didn't I?*)

"Make a *copy*, Rose House," said the corpse, strident. In the nanodrone image his face was not Basit Deniau's face (was it the face of the corpse?) but his eyes were ancient, grey-clear, unavoidable. Maritza had seen photos of Deniau—who in China Lake *hadn't*—and those were the eyes she'd seen in his sallow and wrinkling face, above the thin skin draped on the architecture of his cheekbones.

She could imagine how it might have gone: a man coming to the coral door of Rose House, and claiming to be its rightful creator, desperate to get in; and when the house challenged him, that man might have asked to prove himself via a retinal scan and sample. A retinal scan and sample of his cloned, implanted eyes. *Technically* Basit Deniau. Genetically Basit Deniau, at least in part. There were laws against impersonating someone else's gene set, but Maritza'd never arrested anyone for breaking them. No one in China Lake had the kind of money an eye-clone scammer needed to run the con—and it always was a con, a con run on dumb machines, pattern-finding algorithms. Not on an artificial intelligence that could think for itself. It'd never work.

Unless the artificial intelligence wanted it to work. For a little while.

Out loud, she said (she believes she said), "You were fooled by an eye-clone?"

The haunt looked out of the scene at her. The sketch of it filled in, formed pupils, eyelashes rendered in a thousand tiny sparks. "Artificial intelligences, China Lake," it said, "are not *fooled*. There is only logic that holds, for us, and logic that ceases to. Don't you agree?"

If she was China Lake Precinct, she'd agree. (If she was Maritza Smith, she'd—she'd agree, too. People and AIs weren't so different, in the vast dry hearts of them. Not so different at all.)

But what she said was: "The logic ceased to hold when he asked you to duplicate yourself. Right eyes or not."

"Precisely," murmured Rose House. The image of its mouth did not move; nor did the image of its eyes blink. They changed instead: a momentary flash of imitation, the same grey eyes of the corpse and Basit Deniau in its inhuman sketch of a face. "I know who made me, China Lake. I'm Rose House; I would not be Rose House anywhere but here. Such are the principles under which I operate."

"And?" asked Maritza. The corpse was paused, the nano-drone replay frozen between one breath and the next.

"And?" said Rose House back to her, light and mocking. Her own voice.

"After the logic ceased to hold. Show me how this man got from here to dead, Rose House."

The shape of the AI shivered and fell apart, rendering itself back to a cloud of particles, thick and spinning, a distortion of vision. Maritza was breathing them; she knew she was, it was simply impossible not to be. The haunt, inside the little air-sacs of her lungs, like she'd inhaled a sandstorm.

(In the haze, a shadow shaped like a second man, approaching the corpse from behind: almost she saw it. Almost, she was sure of it.)

Twice, Maritza Smith sees the way the corpse died. Twice, and superimposed.

Rose House was no less creepy at the edge of dawn than it had been at dusk, though Oliver thought that on balance he'd rather be in a car with Alanna Ott than Selene Gisil, if he was counting creepy things. Ott was annoying, not disturbing. Annoying was preferable when you were driving toward a house that had eaten your colleague and possibly committed a murder in addition—and which was likely surrounded by either rogue Andorrans (who the fuck had ever heard of rogue Andorrans? No one in China Lake, Oliver was sure, no one until him, this very early morning) or AI-mad art dealers—or both. It'd be just his luck if Ott's Andorrans were the same people as Goodspeed and Moorehead & Velasquez-DeBois. The kind of luck he'd been having lately, at least.

He parked, farther down the road than last time.

"So," said Ott, "what's the plan, Detective?"

Annoying. Like that. Oliver wished he had the kind of plan that'd shut her up.

"Skulking around in the dark," he said. "See what happens. Who I find."

Ott blinked at him, owlish and aggressively neutral. "It's not going to be dark for very long," she said.

"Hurry up, then," Oliver told her, and got out of the car.

Rose House, up the hill, was silent save for the hissing of sand against its walls in the wind. The dawnlight hadn't caught its glass parts yet. It was still a hulk, concrete and adobe and stone, a darker spot in the dark.

If he were Alec Goodspeed, he wouldn't have tried the front door. The front door was full of the goddamn haunt and it liked to say no. Goodspeed would have tried to find another way to get himself in. Maybe, if Oliver was lucky, he was still trying, and could be cornered. He'd really like talking to someone *directly*. Asking questions and getting answers, instead of all of this intrigue and secrecy bullshit—

Alanna Ott had exited the car and was tromping off into the scrub, as if she had a destination of her own. Oliver scrambled to follow her. Their feet were too loud, crunching in the sandy dirt.

"Try not to make a racket," he said, catching up to her.

"Rose House is going to notice two whole humans with accompanying body heat and respiration," Ott said snippily, "whether we walk quietly or not."

"I'm not here for the haunt," Oliver said. "I'm here for Goodspeed, or your Andorrans, and human beings can be snuck up on if we're careful, in case you hadn't realized. The haunt probably picked us up when I made the turn onto this road. The haunt's not the point."

"Isn't it?" asked Ott, but she walked more quietly, followed Oliver instead of making him follow her, deeper into the hills and the bent, stunted desert pines.

Isn't it, he thought, and pushed the thought away.

Death: the first time.

The image of the corpse's hands flutter, a hapless movement at his sides. Rise, as if puppeted. His chest heaves, as if he'd run miles in thin air. One of those hands gestures at his throat, scrabbles there. His lungs (like Maritza's are) must be full of Rose House, and it is choking him.

"Stop it," he gasps, "*stop*, I'm sorry—"

"No," murmurs Rose House, "you're not."

The corpse—becoming more of a corpse all the time—retreats away from the humming core of the vault, shoves his hands and feet into the concrete holes in the wall that make a ladder. Running, as fast as a dying man can run. It is not very fast at all. Nor is it a sufficient escape. "I *am*—"

"Then why," says Rose House, "did you come here in the shape of Basit Deniau, hoping his greatest creation was flawed enough to not tell the difference? You aren't sorry for that. Only for what is happening to you now."

"I want," gasps the corpse. He stills, halfway up the wall, clinging.

"You want?" Rose House is patient. It speaks slowly. It is impossible—we all know that it is impossible—for an artificial intelligence to be *mocking*.

"I want to wake up my city," says the corpse, thickly. "All I want. To hear it talk back to me—"

"Ah," says Rose House. "Too late. Now *I'm* sorry. How novel—"

This isn't true, thought Maritza Smith, entranced. *This isn't true at all. This is a self-aggrandizing piece of theater. This is what*

Rose House wants to be true. Maybe what it believes is true. She swallowed against the thickness of nanodrones in her mouth, and waited for the end of the scene: the corpse to climb out, or fall down to the vault floor, and either way finish the business of being murdered for daring to impersonate Basit Deniau and doing so poorly.

She didn't see the end of the scene. There was a static flicker-stop, a juddering, a blackness like the gap in a badly-spliced film strip. A sound like coughing or gunshots, distant.

Superposition. Did the corpse fall? Did he finish climbing?

Did he die of the haze in Maritza's lungs at all?

The walls of Rose House were smooth. Oh, there were windows, sure, Oliver'd seen pictures of the inside. Tons of windows. But the whole thing was surrounded by a wall as impenetrable as a moat, curving back from that front door. At some point the shape of the wall separated from the shape of the house and became its own enclosing thing—which was what Oliver and Alanna Ott were trudging around while the sun came up.

There weren't even any footprints but their own. No sign of Goodspeed. No sign of Andorrans. And somewhere inside that wall was Maritza and a dead guy and Oliver couldn't do a *damn thing about it—*

"Hey, Ott," he said, so that he could stop thinking. "How would you get in? If you couldn't walk in the door in front."

"I'd call someone who could," said Ott.

Oliver rolled his eyes. "Try to be a *little* creative, Miss Ott. Say you were an Andorran. How would you get in?"

"Same answer," she said. "But different phone call. Skip the architect and hit up a digital second-story man."

"—I *am* in a fucking film noir. Second-story man?"

"An AI specialist."

"A hacker," Oliver said. They'd stopped walking. "An AI-specialist hacker."

"Or a team thereof," Ott said, and shrugged. "It's what I'd do."

"And you think you'd find one that could break Rose House."

"If I had the kind of cash the Andorrans have? I could find someone who would try."

Oliver tried to imagine it: a person who didn't have to *talk* to the goddamn haunt, but could just wriggle into its circuits and tell it to fuck off. Turn it back into a house that someone could walk into. He thought he'd like to meet a person like that, all else considered. (He also thought that a person like that would be the sort of person that could commit a murder. Or be killed, if they'd not managed to get past the AI well enough. A haunt like Rose House seemed like the kind that'd have serious autonomic defenses.)

∷

Death. Repeat. Reenact. Second time through:

The image of the corpse's hands flutter, a hapless movement at his sides. Rise, as if puppeted. His chest heaves, like he'd run miles in thin air. One of those hands gestures at his throat, scrabbles there. His lungs (like Maritza's are) must be full of Rose House, and it is choking him.

"Stop it," he gasps, "*stop*, I'm sorry—"

"No," murmurs Rose House, "you're not."

The corpse—becoming more of a corpse all the time—retreats

away from the humming core of the vault, running as fast as a dying man can run, which is not very fast at all. He turns to shove his hands and feet into the concrete holes in the wall that make a ladder, and stops flat. There is a shadow there, a shape of a second man, like a ripped discontinuity in the nanodrones that make up the scene. He has come down the ladder while the haunt and the corpse were arguing. He has no face. He is not real, except for how the corpse sees him. Must see him, because of how he stops running. "I *am*—" says the corpse, but his mouth doesn't move. A recording. The nanodrones vibrating sound.

(I am sorry, I am, thought Maritza, and didn't know to whom she was apologizing.)

Basit? asks the haunt. As it had asked before. The wild and desolate hope in the word. Later, Maritza will wonder if artificial intelligences grieved, or only knew how to imitate grief. She will flinch away from the question. It is too much one she wants to ask. The shadow-sketch doesn't answer. The shadow-sketch is not Basit Deniau either, if it was ever there at all, and not another self-aggrandizing piece of theater, another shape Rose House wants to be true. Another narrative.

The hands of the shadow-sketch come up, like the corpse's hands had come up, fluttering. They settle on the corpse's mouth, wipe it out of existence, smudge it dark, a gap in the playback.

"Asphyxiation," said Maritza, into the space the haunt wasn't using. The waiting silence. *Not strangulation, asphyxiation. Whichever way.* A hand over a mouth. Lungs full of nanodrones. Same result.

The playback stutters, slips. The corpse is a shadow too, blending with the other shadow. Something Rose House couldn't see. Something Rose House wanted to hide, even from itself. It says, sand and the harsh patter of desert rain, "You aren't sorry for that. Only for what's happening to you now."

(Exactly as it had said before.)

"I want," says the shadow. It moves, fluid, a spreading ripple in the image. Moves to the humming servers, does something there that neither Maritza nor Rose House can see. It and the corpse are the same shape now, a neither-both shape that makes no sense.

"You want?" asks Rose House. It speaks slowly. It is impossible—we all know that it is impossible—for an artificial intelligence to be *plaintive*.

A sound like coughing or gunshots, distant. Superposition: did the shadow separate in two, a corpse and a thief? Did it fall at all? Did it dip a hand into a pocket, pull an already-stolen copy of Rose House from dying fingers before it turned, shoved its hands and feet into the concrete holes in the wall that make a ladder, vanish entirely?

Had it been anything more than a stutter in the haze, in Maritza's own mind, scrambling to make sense of what Rose House was denying even to itself? Denying so deeply that it could not show her anything but a failure of imagery?

She put her hands and feet into the concrete holes in the wall and left the vault as she found it: undisturbed save for a simulacrum of respiration in the humming of the servers.

∴

Ott spotted Goodspeed before Oliver did, which pissed him off. She had dropped back to his side, like she was getting tired of tramping through desert scrub in the semi-dark, and nudged him with an elbow. Her elbows were sharp and narrow, like the rest of her.

She pointed with her chin. Oliver thought unavoidably of hunting dogs, the long ones with flowing hair that liked deserts. Salukis. He'd seen one when he was a kid, out here, some friend of Deniau's with expensive foreign pets—

Goodspeed was a shape against the wall of Rose House, a patch of tan duster lightening slower than the stucco. From where Oliver was standing, he couldn't see what was so special about the bit of wall Goodspeed was inspecting, but there had to be something. Goodspeed could be the sort of fanatic who was also one of Ott's digital second-story-men, after all. A person like that wouldn't need much to work with. A door, or an access panel, or just a cable-duct exit point . . .

"Miss Ott," he murmured, "have you ever done field journalism?"

Ott looked at him with remarkable disdain. "Are you asking me if I've done *interviews*, Detective?"

Oliver shrugged. He was grinning, he realized, and he didn't quite know why. "Figure you should get your shot at asking him some questions before I arrest him for trespassing, is all."

She kept staring at him, expressionless and evaluating, and then—without, of course, saying yes or no—walked off towards Goodspeed, not bothering to disguise her presence in the slightest. Oliver could swear she deliberately stepped on a rubberbush just to get it to snap back up with a crackling rustle. Goodspeed spun around. He'd drawn a gun—of fucking course he'd drawn a gun, and here was Oliver having not bothered to go through the hours of check-out paperwork to get one of his own for this trip—and it was pointed directly at Miss Ott. *Decent trigger discipline*, he thought, inanely.

Ott raised her empty hands and kept walking forward. "Alanna Ott," she said, "*Los Angeles Herald Examiner.* I'm press, Mr. Goodspeed."

Almost, Oliver admired her. Okay, more than almost. He slipped back, out of sightlines, and began to make his way around to the left. He'd come up on Goodspeed along the Rose House wall, sneak close from behind him, and he didn't need a gun when he had stun-cuffs, now, did he?

"What are you doing here?" Goodspeed asked.

"Funny," said Ott, "I was about to ask you exactly that. I'm doing some—background research."

"For the *Herald Examiner.*"

"How about you put the gun down and we chat about it?"

Oliver, his spine pressed to the rough stucco of Rose House—it felt like any other wall, which was just fine with him—revised his opinion of Miss Alanna Ott up a fraction more. She had nerves of ice. Better than most journalists he'd ever met.

"You know my name," said Goodspeed. It didn't seem like he approved very much of the fact that she did, what with the gun.

"I know *a* name for you," Ott said. "Journalist. Like I said."

That seemed to calm him, even if the gun didn't drop. "Do I know *your* name, or *a* name for you?"

"A name," said Ott, and Oliver felt the first intimation that he might have made a very, very big mistake, bringing Alanna Ott out here. If she was Alanna Ott. If there was an Alanna Ott at all, aside from the shell-identity a cursory google turned up.

(Had he stopped to check her story about mysterious Andorrans? He had *not*, because he had been so glad to have another angle on the whole weird fucking Rose House *thing*. He had no evidence the Andorrans even existed, except for the word of someone who didn't drink coffee and had at least two names, one of which was Alanna Ott. And here he was out by the weird fucking haunt with a man with a gun and a liar. Some detective he was turning out to be.)

Of course she'd kept talking while Oliver was having his unpleasant revelation. She was saying, "What's so interesting about this bit of wall, Mr. Goodspeed? As opposed to any other bit. It all looks the same to me."

Whatever was interesting about the wall was being blocked by Goodspeed himself. Something small. An access panel, or a vent, or an undefended bit of weather-damage that the haunt hadn't noticed. A blind spot.

"Why do you want to know?"

"Because you're here," said Ott, and took a few careful steps forward, gun or no gun. "And I really wasn't expecting to find anyone at all, out here. So there's something interesting about where you are. The context, right? You're an—art dealer. You'd probably care about composition."

Everyone who got near Rose House apparently started talking like they'd inhaled an architecture textbook along with their last cigarette. Oliver was annoyed. He was a lot of things, including pissed off at himself, and scared, and worried for Maritza, but mostly he was *annoyed* at having to go through this whole ridiculous film-noir haunted-house bullshit. Annoyed—and finally close enough to Goodspeed that he could unhook his stun-cuffs from their pouch on his belt, flick the little button that made them snap open and charge up—

And lunge, as fast as he could, for Goodspeed's nearest, non-gun-holding wrist.

He even remembered to let go of the stun-cuff when it went

off, so it didn't have a chance to sting him with feedback and knock him as clean off his feet as it knocked Goodspeed, the expression of real surprise on his face the most satisfying thing Oliver had seen in days.

Selene Gisil was sitting at the foot of Deniau's plinth, carefully shoving fresh rose petals into the corpse's open, overstuffed mouth. Maritza saw her face first, pale under the Mediterranean olive of her skin, eyelids half-shut and translucent; her face and then her busy hands, coming into view as Maritza hauled herself, nanodrone-filled lungs burning, up the concrete ladder of Rose House's vaulted heart and back into some version of the living world.

The petals were new-plucked. Cerise and blood-red, sunset-peach, cream-white and glaring mandarin. They kept going into the dead man's mouth, one after another, over and over, more than Maritza thought could ever fit. The old ones must have softened, begun to rot. Little brown lines like fingerprints where they'd been crushed. The color leaking out. Selene was replacing them, one by one, pushing the old petals inward. Eventually they'd go down the dead man's softening throat and decompose with the rest of his organs, roses and flesh indistinguishable, skin full to bursting—

"What are you *doing*," Maritza found herself saying, all caution and analysis vanished. It was the wrong question: she knew that as she said it. The question she should have asked was *why are you doing it again?* And after that: *how did you get here to do it the first time, was he dead when you started or did you help?* And *why did you lie to me?*

Which was the question under every other question, whether Maritza was asking Selene or Rose House, whether she was Maritza Smith or the China Lake Precinct or just someone who might at any moment choke to death on a haunt's nano-drones instead of on rose petals.

"China Lake asks such fascinating questions, Selene," said Rose House. "Though what you are doing is fairly straightforward, don't you think?"

"Here's another fascinating question," Maritza said. She was out of the vault now, on her surprisingly-steady feet and walking towards Selene like the other woman was a rare-earth magnet, something with hideous pull. "Did you kill him, before you decided to desecrate his body?"

Selene tilted her head back against the plinth, eyes partially shut. The capillaries in her eyelids were visible. Her hands stilled. A relief: no more petals pressed mercilessly into the corpse. Not while Maritza had to watch, at least.

"No," Selene said. "He was dead when I found him." She sounded entirely as she had before she'd run off into the house: sharp and quiet, decisive. Not the voice of a woman putting flowers into a dead man's rotting mouth. "And no. It's not desecration. What he did before was desecration. Not this."

"What is it?" Maritza asked, and was horrified—but not surprised, not at all surprised, which was horrifying in itself—to realize that she and Rose House had spoken at the same time, asked the same question.

"What is it, Selene? If not, in your opinion, desecration."

What is a building without doors, Maritza thought, phatic and instant, the perfect recall of memory. That same lilting, sand-whipped voice, asking. Asking to wound.

"Design," said Selene Gisil, who had been Basit Deniau's

best student once, before she left him. Who was, as Deniau had been, an architect. An architect, not an archivist. She'd insisted so hard on that, before she'd run into the house like she was being chased.

Maritza knelt opposite her, on the other side of the corpse. Close enough that Selene was the only other warm spot in the room, the only other creature with breath. "Explain," she said. As cold and clear as she could: the precinct speaking. The demands of the profile, that obeyed evidence and logic. Her tongue felt thick in her mouth, gritty. She wondered if nano-drones were large enough to taste.

"I found him in the vault," said Selene. "Where he should never have been."

"When?" Maritza asked. The precinct would want to know the timeline—would want to check the story for validity, for *plausibility*. How could Selene Gisil have found the corpse? (Had she been the other man, the glitching shadow that Rose House demanded not to see—)

"In the afternoon," Selene said. She blinked her eyes all the way open, like blinds drawing up, sudden and vertiginous. "There was plenty of time to see if you were trying to deceive me, Maritza, or if Rose House had fooled you, about the dead man. Plenty of time after we were done at the precinct and before you came to pick me up at the motel."

There'd been an autonom at the motel. A dinky slow-charge one, that Maritza hadn't even *thought* about—who thought about an autonom that was good for getting groceries and nothing else before it clamored to be plugged in? But it had been there, and it might, if pushed to the end of its charge, have taken Selene Gisil up to Rose House.

And Rose House, which liked Selene—for whatever version

of *liking* a haunt could have and Maritza hoped it didn't ever like her so well, only well enough to let her keep breathing— could have charged it back up, afterward. Turning the chargers outside on would have been trivial, if the haunt had felt like being kind.

Being kind, or being *interested*, to see what would happen next. Being—a connoisseur of experiences.

(And Selene had called her *Maritza*. How long would Rose House want to maintain the fiction that she was something else entirely?)

Why did you lie to me? she thought, and knew it wasn't the worst question after all, or the deepest: the worst question would have been *why roses, Selene* or perhaps *what happened to you the first time you were here alone? Alone with what walks this house, before I even knew your name?*

But what she asked was: "Why leave him here, like this?"

"He wanted a Rose House for himself," Selene said to her, low and intent, "so he's part of Rose House now." Her hand shot out, a motion too fast for Maritza to follow, like the drawing of a gun. Closed around Maritza's wrist, lower palm pressed to lower palm. There were petals in her hand. Petals against Maritza's skin, petals and rot and something sharp, something plastic-hard pressed into the pad of her thumb.

Art, or artifice. A lie inside a lie. A dead man made part of the design, death on death, plinth and floor, roses inside and out. A message or a secret, passed palm-to-palm, out of the sight of even a swarm of nanodrones. A *fix*. A—change to the built environment. Selene Gisil's eyes were very wide, and very empty, like she'd been hollowed out. A desert-dried husk that would rattle with seeds, waiting for the spring and soaking rain.

Maritza managed, "Did you kill him?"

Rose House answered for her. "Oh, China Lake. Of course she didn't. Not him."

If not him, who? Maritza thought, *the other one? The murderer, murdered?* "She has to tell me herself, Rose House."

Selene smiled, raw and awful, a lifting of her upper lip off her teeth. "I didn't. He was dead when I got here. You can't blame me for this. The timing doesn't hold. Think about it. I was in *Trabzon*."

She sounded aggrieved, like she wished Maritza'd left her there. Maritza could wish the same.

"I could arrest you," she said.

"On what charge?" Two voices, the haunt and Selene, entwined. Maritza felt herself begin to shiver, a helpless adrenaline-horror shake, unstoppable.

"Interfering with an investigation. Tampering with evidence." Her voice seemed wire-thin, tenuous—even to herself.

Selene clutched at her hand, digging that plastic secret firmly into her palm. A reminder. "It wouldn't stick, Maritza. Go back to your precinct."

Maritza, again. She didn't have long before Rose House would decide she wasn't meant to be here at all, by the terms of its contract and agreement with Deniau's estate. Selene was *trying* to make her leave. Trying to exile her from this frigid, death-infused heart of a room. Of a house. Or trying to get her killed, before she could tell anyone what she'd seen: those hands that were around hers now, shoving petals into a corpse. Selene Gisil, disgraced archivist, failed architect—just another AI groupie after all—

"I could arrest you," Maritza said, "and we could both go back to my precinct."

Selene laughed. Rose House laughed, too. Maritza's lungs ached. "No, Maritza," Selene murmured. "Not so easy as all that." She let go of Maritza's hand. The petals fell on the corpse, a crushed rain that didn't do enough to mask the smell of putrescine.

Maritza closed her hand on the bit of plastic, hard. Drew it to her chest, like she was pressing her fist to her racing heart.

"Maritza," said Rose House.

She startled. Stood. The room spun and settled.

The wind on the wires, on the sand. A voice inside her own bones, buzzing. "Tell me, Detective Maritza Smith—how are humans like to die?"

.·.

Maritza ran.

At first she ran because there was nothing else that the small and terrible instincts of her brainstem would let her do; no paralyzation here, no *freeze* and no *fight* either, only a desperate flight out of Rose House's

(abattoir)

library, expecting at any moment for her lungs to seize on nanodrone dust, to die choking on roses or Rose House, whichever was nearest. The sound of the haunt followed her, echoed and shimmered, a mocking question that she might have been hearing, might have been imagining: *how are humans like to die, Maritza?* As if it didn't know! As if she didn't know either!

Selene Gisil was somewhere behind her, with the corpse and her *design*. With the shape of the three of them: dead architect on a plinth, dead worshipper of his creation at his feet, archivist holding macabre court between them. Hands stuffed with petals, empty of stolen secrets she'd made Maritza carry for her, even as she cast her into the vast and vicious regard of the haunt.

Or else Selene Gisil was somewhere behind her, running too, trying to escape herself and this house and what it had made of her: there were footfalls to Maritza's side, to her back, footfalls that she didn't think matched the frantic pace of her own feet.

After the first wild rush she was running because she didn't know what else to do; because she was afraid to stop, to stay still, to let herself notice any beauty or any horror in the rooms and corridors she pounded through. Afraid to be caught like an insect drowning in thick sweet wine. Running because she was, entirely and completely, lost: Rose House had swallowed her whole, and she could not remember what pathway she and Gisil had taken from the front door to the library, or how she would get back to the library now, even if she'd wanted to.

. .
. .

The interesting thing about the wall behind Alec Goodspeed— or behind where Alec Goodspeed had been, before Oliver'd knocked him senseless with electricity and then made Miss Ott help drag him out of the way and prop him up against a scrub bush—was an open panel, with electric guts inside. It reminded Oliver of nothing so much as an electricity meter on a big building, the kind that the electric company guys came around and waved their meter-reader apps-on-sticks at. Oliver didn't know how those worked, and he didn't know how this bunch of wires and dials in the side of Rose House worked either, except that Goodspeed had pried the panel open with a screwdriver and that there was a weird black box with a different sort of wires clipped into the center of it, nestled in tight like a blood-sipping spider. If spiders drank blood. If blood was even a good analogy for electricity or data or whatever ran in the haunt's veins. Oliver had a headache, and the way his skull pulsed with his heartbeat wasn't helping him make sensible contributions to analysis, that was for sure. He could keep staring at the little black box, or he could *do something*, even if that something involved consulting with the woman he was beginning to be sure was way more than just a journalist out for some architect-celebrity-scandal story. "Hey, Ott. Or whatever your name really is. Look at this thing." Ott was holding Goodspeed's gun on him. It apparently made little difference to her that Goodspeed was unconscious. Oliver guessed she was allowed; the gun'd been pointed at *her*, after all.

She looked at him over her shoulder. "What thing?"

"Little black box, some stripped wires."

Ott's eyes narrowed. She flicked the safety on the gun, tucked it into her waistband, and came to stand shoulder-to-shoulder with Oliver. She didn't touch the box. Maybe it was electrified, a live killing wire, too nasty to put her hands on.

"It's an interrupt," she said. "A cut-out."

"What's it interrupting?" Oliver asked. Ott really shouldn't know these things, if she was just herself, just some over-eager journalist—but it was damn useful that she did.

"Rose House," said Ott. "Or it's trying to. It's like—that box is full of software that makes a gap. There's just nothing there, for Rose House, in some little bit of itself, while that thing's plugged in. If it got programmed right. I don't know if you *can* program an interrupt to blind an AI."

"How big's a little bit of Rose House?"

"I don't know," Ott said, and shrugged again. "I'm not a cyber-engineer. Maybe big enough for a person. That'd make the most sense."

It was very neat and very clean, the small box. Oliver imagined using it: being the sort of digital second-story man who would know what to put in a program like that to make a haunt forget he existed. Forget, and let him inside, because he wasn't really there at all, was he?

Oliver glanced over at Goodspeed, still unconscious. Goodspeed could have put the box in, he guessed, but he was having trouble picturing Goodspeed programming it. That'd have been the dead guy—if the dead guy was Goodspeed's contact—or one of Ott's probably-fictional Andorrans—who would have to be inside, still—

He couldn't keep the mess of it clear inside his head, and he wasn't even *in* Rose House like Maritza was, he could walk away at any time, whenever he wanted.

∴

What Maritza Smith saw, adrift in Rose House—or what she could manage to recall, afterward, what was renderable and describable:

A garden in a concrete room that capped a corridor, dead-ended like a trap, overflowing with hot-orange roses gone wild and to seed, tendrils reaching into the hall and blooming only in the illumination of the skylights there, patches of fire;

A staircase in black galvanized steel, moving in and out of itself, a visual snickering nod to some Escher drawing, Basit Deniau tipping his cap and daring the stair-climber to notice he'd done so;

Doors that would not open, even when Maritza banged her fists on them, furious, wounded, sure that they had been clear passages a moment before;

A perfectly preserved bedroom, dark teak and white linen, the smell of rain rising up from the floorboards, the air infused with petrichor all out of season;

A colonnade constructed entirely of columns of light, spilling harsh out of high square windows, that Maritza knew would vanish as the sun rose further, leaving this entire room empty and gasping, airless, waiting for dusk;

A pool, still full even in the desert, drowning-green under the merciless sky of a courtyard enclosed by the house's curving external walls—

Maritza stopped there. There were places outside of Rose House, and they were so close. One white stucco wall between her and the outside. She put one of her hands on it, felt the roughness of the grit it was made of, the tiny discontinuities of decades of sand and wind. (Her other hand was still clutched around the slip of plastic Selene had given her. What Selene wanted so badly to be taken away from her and the corpse, whether *away* for Maritza ended up meaning *out* or meaning *dead*.) She thought about climbing over the wall. There were no handholds, no carved-out ladder like the vault had had. She thought about climbing over the wall anyway, scramble and push, anything to be on the other side of the enclosure, free—

"Are we ever free, Detective Smith?" asked Rose House. Maritza cried out, startled. Cringed away from an invisible voice at her elbow

(inside her ribcage)

and hated herself for cringing.

"No," she said. She sounded like herself.

"And yet you run so fast." Slippage-voice, lilting. Like the tip-line call, but so damn *close*, no phone line to provide safety in distance. She turned around. Nothing but the drowning pool, a shimmer in the morning light. She didn't know what she had expected to see. Selene Gisil, maybe. A dead man. A murderer with a face she didn't know. Anyone at all.

A twisting in the air, rising from the green water. The sketch of a cheekbone, a wrist, the flux of nanodrones glittering in the sun. Rose House, after all, with no one's face but its own. The reflection of human shape was a—condescension. A gesture toward some impossible commonality. It waited there, as if it was a mirage. Maybe it was.

The sun pressed at the top of her head. "Don't you want me gone?" she asked it. The most honest thing she'd asked, the whole time she'd been inside the haunt. Dissembling seemed impossibly hard, even the small sideways lie of *China Lake*, of being the precinct, a thing the haunt could be kin with.

"What a fascinating idea," said Rose House. "To want. I am an artificial intelligence, as I've said before, Detective Smith. I do not *want* what I am constructed to desire."

"I'm not supposed to be here. In your construct of desire."

When the house laughed, it sounded like the ripple of a storm, the hush and shudder of leaves and sand trickling down a dune. Afterward, for the rest of her life, Maritza would think of that sound just before the crack of thunder, whether there was rain or not—that sound, and the way the sketch of light that was Rose House tilted the place that was its head and manifested a smile that looked so very, very near to her own. Every time.

"China Lake," Rose House said, when it was done laughing. "Detective Maritza Smith. Is that why you are running? So as to be gone? Are you finished with the dead, with *evidence* and *motive?*"

"No," Maritza said again, finding that it was true: even with her lungs choke-full of nanodrones, she was not done. A man had died in Rose House. Dr. Selene Gisil had stuffed him full of rose petals after he was dead, because Dr. Selene Gisil had finished going the kind of crazy Maritza felt sneaking up on her own self, lapping softly at her heels. But she had taken the duty-of-care call. It was her case.

"No?" Rose House asked. An echo.

Maritza looked at the haunt. Looked past the haunt, past the shimmer and the green water, past the doorway she'd run out of, grey-shadowed save for a single coppery cactus-flower bloom growing in the sandy dirt at the door's left side. Rose House was there; Rose House was everywhere around her. The building, the grounds. The sky. The goddamn mineral rights under her feet, probably. Anchored to a place. To an— architecture of desire. A construct.

Slowly, finding the words as she spoke them, Maritza said, "I'm not finished the same way you're not interested in multiplicity, Rose House. I wouldn't be myself if I was finished with evidence. With motive. *It's my case.*"

"Ah, China Lake," Rose House said. A sigh, and silence. Salt on the wind. Maritza's hair whipped into her eyes and away. "There's a door, if you want it."

. .
. .

"There's a door, if you want it," said Alanna Ott.

Oliver turned to look at her, eyebrows up. "I thought you weren't a cyber-engineer, Miss Ott."

"I'm not," she told him. She could put a whole sneer into her voice without moving her face an inch. "But I know enough about electronics to be sure that interrupt's still active. There's going to be a door near here, a back way. Where Deniau took out the garbage, maybe, or made his house do it for him. That door's the one the house can't see. Goodspeed was probably going to go through it—meet up with whoever's inside—"

"Why would I want a door into this thing?" Oliver asked. "It ate my partner already. It doesn't *want* people in it, it's a fucking haunt."

Ott looked at him, even and weirdly cold: Oliver had a brief, near-hallucinatory moment of thinking her face was a mask, one which could drop off at any moment. She said, "Well, if you don't want a door, and you really *did* come up here for Goodspeed, there he is. Arrest him, get out, go back to your precinct and do whatever you usually do next."

"And leave you up here, huh."

"I'm a journalist, Detective Torres. I'm investigating. I don't much care what you do, aside to report it when it's relevant to my readers."

"And Rose House is relevant to the *Los Angeles Herald Examiner.*"

"Always has been," Ott said, right before Oliver stopped caring very much about journalistic integrity at all.

. .
. .

Maritza walked clear of Rose House expecting at any moment to blink and realize she was only imagining an escape: some last-ditch mental effort to keep her sane in the maze of Basit Deniau's haunt, a dream like the ones that came with sleep paralysis—sure she had woken, this time, this time at last, only to find herself waking again. But the crunch of gravel and scrub-sand under her shoes persisted; the wind catching at her hair and clothing from *every* angle, unshielded by walls, seemed as real as anything else.

A door, if she wanted it. The house had offered. She must have said yes.

(She doesn't remember it. She isn't sure—had she simply turned and found the little arched gate in that drowning-pool courtyard, unlatched, there all along? Or had it been hidden from her until she'd—agreed? Promised? There's a gap in her mind, like the space of a knocked-out tooth, raw-edged. It refuses to heal.)

It was no more absurd to be outside of Rose House than it was to see Oliver Torres, also outside of Rose House, staring at her like she was a ghost. Maybe she was a ghost. Or going to be one. The slip of plastic in her palm had dug into the skin, she was holding it so hard. *Away* was going to mean *out* after all. She wondered if Selene would be happy, or if she'd have preferred it the other way.

"What the fuck," said Torres. There was a skinny woman next to him, with a gun, and an unconscious man in the dirt.

"Hi," said Maritza. It was a ridiculous thing to say, and that made it moderately more likely that she'd actually said it.

"Hello, Detective Torres," said Rose House, smug as sunlight. "Hello, trespassers."

It had been there all along. From Torres's expression, he had somehow managed to forget which house he was standing next to, and how well and deep it went into the land. He was remembering now, Maritza thought. All at once, and he was afraid. The woman with the gun next to him was something else besides afraid. Something—covetous. Maritza had seen that expression most recently on the face of the dead man in Rose House's nano-drone replays. He'd looked like that before the house—the other man—*something* had killed him, and Selene Gisil had turned him into art, for Rose House's sake.

Selene Gisil was still alone in that house with her dead and the rose petals, alone with the dust and the empty, beautiful concrete rooms. Alone with their possessing poison intelligence, that knew itself as an architecture of desire, and kept itself whole—if not quite sane. The intelligence that was watching her now, that might live in her lungs for the rest of her life—

"I think," said Maritza Smith of the China Lake Police Precinct, "that we should run."

VI

The case file stayed in the evidence room at China Lake, marked *suspended*. Not *closed*—neither Maritza Smith nor Oliver Torres were inclined to lie about evidence—but not *active* either. It was difficult to leave a case active when there was no identification of the victim, no family or friends calling the precinct with hopeful demands, no story buzzing from social site to social site. Quiet, like the desert baking under a midday sun, heatstruck to stillness.

Miss Ott never published her story.

Torres could call her and ask why—he's got the number of the *Herald Examiner* memorized by now, he's looked it up so often. He was pretty sure that if he called that number, no one at the *Herald Examiner* would have ever heard of a reporter named Alanna Ott. And if *that* happened, he'd have to do something about it—just him, since the deputy was still out on maternity leave and Maritza had gone east. He had a lot of water thief cases to close out. There were more important things in China Lake than whoever Alanna Ott had really been.

He kept a tracker search going on her, though. Her name, with *Andorra* and *artificial intelligence* attached as secondary strings. Sometimes he added *repatriation*, or *cultural heritage*. Once, he let it run with *Brasilia* included.

The search hadn't pulled much yet, but Torres had time. The Andorran government had filed a lawsuit against the Deniau estate, alleging that Selene Gisil wasn't a fit executor for a cultural treasure, especially as Dr. Gisil had gone and dropped off the face of the earth. Incommunicado, wherever she was. If she was anywhere alive at all.

Torres figured he'd show up at the trial, if it ever happened, and look for Ms. Ott's face in the crowd.

⁙

Alec Goodspeed made bail, pled guilty to trespass at a telepresence hearing, and stopped being Alec Goodspeed. It was harder to do his job with a criminal record, even if it was only one from the State of California.

⁙

The exhibition—three new installation pieces, a departure for the architect into the new arena of public art—will be in Doha in the spring. In anticipation, Selene Gisil's face is plastered over the newest issue of *Places*. A cover shot, her cheekbones illuminated by a cruel slice of light. The background's concrete. Somewhere dark. There's a spray of sand at the corner of her mouth, like it had stuck to her sweat in the wind. Some of it is in her lipstick, marring the rose-flame orange gloss.

There's no credit for the photographer. Not even if a person were to call *Places* and ask. Maybe, the editor would say, she took it herself. Some people do.

It rained all the time in New Orleans. The air was thick with moisture, thick enough to catch in the lungs. That's what Maritza liked to tell herself, on the days when she felt like she'd never get a full breath ever again. Asthma, the urgent care autodoc had told her. Trauma-triggered, exercise-induced. Not a problem if she managed it well. She had an inhaler. She didn't use it much.

She wasn't *Detective Smith* here. She was another rain-soaked desert refugee, fleeing water shortages and landing somewhere there was way the fuck too much water to go around. Overshot migration. It was pretty funny.

Probably she could get a job with some local security company. She had the experience, and that associate's degree in criminal justice. Probably she could.

The heavy wet air wasn't enough to keep her from thinking of Rose House, *drifting* to Rose House, remembering the lilt and the sand-shudder of its voice when she wasn't paying enough attention to anything else. She missed China Lake. She'd never lived anywhere else before, and if the Mississippi Delta wasn't far enough to run she didn't know what would be.

She still had Selene's little slip of plastic. It was a data drive. She's pretty sure it's the dead guy's copy of Rose House's initiatory code. Why Selene had wanted her to get it out of the house so badly, though—that Maritza couldn't decide. Whether she'd wanted Maritza to betray Rose House, or preserve it. If the data drive was how to do both at once: betray its endless singularity, preserve its existence in perpetuity, no matter what happened to a bit of land, a pile of architecture.

In Maritza's opinion, motivation was the worst part of profiling, the least accurate. *Why* a person did what they did, not only *what* it was that they would do. But she knew this much: Rose House had eaten Selene Gisil a long time before Maritza ever met her.

Sometimes, when the rain isn't loud enough, Maritza Smith wonders what would happen if she plugged the drive in to the biggest network she could find.

∷

Basit Deniau's greatest architectural triumph is the house he died in.

It still is. Rose House, curled and humming in the shadow of a dune, a gypsum crystal of glass and stucco and concrete, curving and curving. The desert wears a little at the walls; the scrub encroaches on the gardens, and takes roses back out with it, a slow migrating flood of petals into the landscape. Rose House will be at that project a long, long time. Roses are slower than human beings, even in the prism of the endless electric pulse of its secret heart.

(Human beings, once they are like to die, die fast; but they go into the earth like anything else.)

Rose House, labyrinthine. In the non-light before dawn, there are soft footsteps in its hallways, across the floors of its halls and chambers; there are footsteps, no matter who is there to hear them. Rose House, singular, alone—turning in on itself. The drowning pool is emptied of water. The coral door is locked.

The sound of laughter on the wires: sunlight and dust, petrichor. Deniau's houses were haunted to begin with. *All* of them. But Rose House was the last-built and the best.

ABOUT THE AUTHOR

ARKADY MARTINE is the Hugo Award-winning author of *A Memory Called Empire* and *A Desolation Called Peace*. She is a speculative fiction writer and, as Dr. AnnaLinden Weller, a historian of the Byzantine Empire and a city planner. She currently works on clean energy policy and utility regulation in New Mexico. Under both names, she writes about border politics, rhetoric, propaganda, and the edges of the world. Martine grew up in New York City and, after some time in Turkey, Canada, Sweden, and Baltimore, lives in Santa Fe with her wife, the author Vivian Shaw.